CHANCED

Internet Famous Collection, 5

MAREE MOON

———

Editing & Proofing:
Dr. Plot Twist
Cam Johns & Dominique Laura.
Cover Design: Touch Creations Graphics
Collection Concept : Rewritten Fairytales

———

CHAPTER ONE

Mr. 3B Hottie

MINA

"Hey, Mina. Are you ready yet? I don't want to miss our flights." My best friend of over ten years stands in the doorway of my room, tapping her foot impatiently.

"Almost done, Mandy." I shove the last shirt into my suitcase while scanning the room for any missing item. "Give me a sec."

"I don't know how you can wait until the last minute to pack every time," Mandy complains as she slumps down on the bed next to the suitcase. "I started mine last month."

"A month ago?" I crunch my nose at that. "How do you remember what you packed? I would have to remove everything and pack them all over again."

"That's exactly what happened," Mandy informs me. "Packed and repacked several times. Maybe seven or eight times before exams started. Then one more time yesterday after my last final. My brain was fried, and I couldn't remember what I put in there." She flops back on the pillows. "My finals were brutal."

"I know what you mean," I say as I close my small carry-on. "I'm ready. Let's go."

Mandy props herself up on her elbows. "Where is the other bag?"

"What other bag?"

"Is that all you are taking for a vacation? That can't possibly be enough for two and a half weeks."

"I am making a pit stop at Mom's before I go on vacation," I say as I haphazardly lock the suitcase. "I will grab some other stuff there."

"I thought you said you weren't going to do the parent thing this vacation."

"Up until last night, I wasn't going to. Then I was advised I had no choice on the matter."

"What do you mean?" Mandy throws her feet over the edge of the mattress and sits up while straightening out the covers of my not-so-perfectly made bed.

"Mom changed my tickets without notifying me. Now I have a two-day layover in New York."

"Oh, wow! That's aggressive!" After rearranging my pillow on its side, Mandy asks, "Is everything okay? No medical issues?"

"No, not that I am aware of, but who knows what my mother is thinking." I drag my feet to the front door with Mandy in tow. After locking it, Mandy checks it twice. "It's locked!" I loop my fingers around her wrist and drag her outside.

When we reach the car, I place my carry-on in the backseat next to her oversized suitcase. "What's with the massive luggage? Aren't you going home to visit your family?" I ask as Mandy comes over for a selfie.

"It's Christmas vacation with the family," she replies, angling the phone above our heads for optimal angles. "I need extra space to bring back all the gifts."

My eyes flicker up to the time on the corner of her phone. *Shit!* My flight leaves in an hour. I tug her hand, disrupting her filter application. She never posts anything without running it through a beauty app. "Move, Mandy. I am so late... I'm not even checked in!"

She snorts and enters the car while I round the front to the driver's side, fretting about the time crunch. I get all flustered as Mandy aims the camera phone at me again.

"Stop it!" I shout, slamming the car door and wiggling the phone out of my back pocket with some difficulty. After handing her my phone, I insert the key in the ignition. "Check in for me while I drive. Please?" Luckily, it's a ten-minute drive over to the parking lot, and there's a shuttle that takes us to the terminal in a few minutes.

"Only because I love you." She abandons her phone in the cup holder and rummages through my backpack for my items while I haul ass. "I don't like people cutting into my social time."

I roll my eyes and step on the accelerator. "You have time to kill after I board. Your plane only leaves in a few hours."

"True. I can vlog about how unprepared you are."

"Not if you ever want a ride again."

I skip check-in and run to the TSA line with a full bladder, which is not fun. My heart sinks at the sight of the enormous line. *I'm so going to miss my flight, and Mom's going to think I did it on purpose. And I have to pee.*

I look down at my ticket, holding on to my last bit of hope. In bold letters, I see the words TSA-pre, which means I can take the shorter line and not have to remove my shoes unless they beep.

With my luck though, they'll most definitely beep. Where the metal in my heels is, I have no idea, but it's annoying.

When it's my turn, I quickly hop around on a one-socked foot, removing my last shoe, and throw all my belongings into a plastic bin, not taking any chances on getting tagged for inspection.

I should have taken my bra off. *Crap.* If the damn machine beeps at me, I'm going to piss on it. *Not literally.* But I'll be pissed off.

I glance up at the scanner, and the TSA agent looks at my disheveled hair and shoeless feet and rolls his eyes, gesturing for me to pass. "They're going to close the gate soon."

"Even God doesn't want my mom to get annoyed," I mumble to myself as I drag my container down the roller, inserting one shoe and skipping to the end where another agent shakes her head at me.

I force a smile, thread my arm through my jacket, and limp out of the area with the heel of my foot hanging over the back of my shoe, before she snaps at me to keep the express line moving.

With my sleeve dragging on the floor, I awkwardly speed-walk toward my gate. *If this isn't cardio, I don't know what is,* I think to myself as I adjust my hair and tie my shoelaces while my alarm clock buzzes incessantly.

The black plaque with the white letters signals my arrival. *I made it.* I take a quick selfie and send it to Mandy with the caption. "I MADE IT!"

Flipping applications, I thumb through my emails for my boarding pass on my cell phone while crossing my legs and awkwardly hiding what Mandy calls a pee shuffle. Suddenly, I hear a slam. The door to the gate just closed.

After nearly dropping my phone, I launch myself toward the gate, shouting, "Wait! I'm on that flight."

One of the agents at the gate raises her arm to stop the other one from leaving. "Why didn't you board if this is your flight? We thought you were just taking pictures."

"I'm sorry. I noticed the door was still open and thought I had time. I'm a vlogger, and my followers like to see the travel stages." She doesn't have to know I don't have that many followers.

The agent takes pity on me and runs me in.

"Thank you!" I know how rare it is to re-open the door. I rush down the jet bridge. Luckily, I'm seated in the front, so I don't have to do the air aisle walk of shame. I just have to find out where to put my carry-on. The attendants haven't closed the overhead bins yet, and it looks jammed up there, but luckily there's a spot near my seat.

Score! Still winded from the hustle over, I heave the bag in the air to place it in the compartment.

Oh, no! The bag slips out of my hand and slides downward onto the man in the seat under it. He catches it just as it hits him in the head.

I gasp as I reach for my bag, still hovering over his head. "I am so sorry, are you hurt?"

"No." His response comes out in a strong voice, not very gentle. "I'm fine."

Great, cause I'm mortified. "You're in the drop zone... It slipped, I really—" *Why isn't he releasing the bag?*

"Let me get this for you," he says in a softer tone, but still annoyed. I don't blame him. The hard plastic wheel had smacked him on the forehead.

With cheeks still shooting flames all the way to my ears, I step to the side and let him out of his seat.

He's very tall and has to lower his head to keep from hitting it on the overhead. He easily secures the bag in the bin, turns to me, and flashes me his swoon-worthy smile. "Is there anything else I can put up here for you?"

The buzz zings all the way to my toes, rendering me speechless. I pass him my backpack and smile. This man is gorgeous. Tall, muscular, and just—wow.

Holy hotness it's scorching in here. It should be illegal to look this fine in public. I'd rather stick him behind a screen and gawk at him without having to form words.

He looks back at me when he is done closing the lever to the storage, flat-out catching me admiring his physique. His eyes roam down to my lips, then back up to my eyes. "Need help finding your seat?"

I need help finding my brain.

I turn completely red. All of me, splotched arms and all. It's so embarrassing being caught checking someone out, especially someone as smoldering as him.

"You okay?" *Why does he keep talking to me?*

I clear my throat, dragging the words I swallowed back up. "Uh—"

The loudspeaker comes on. *Saved by the so-called bell.* I flee to my seat, just behind him, and strap myself so I don't lunge forward and sniff his hair or something. I brave a peek upward to check if he does the same.

He is still standing and grinning down at me.

I return the smile, still flush from being caught, still unable to formulate words, still gawking like an idiot at the beautiful man with the perfect white teeth.

Thankfully, he takes his seat, leaving me to wallow in silence.

Well, not technically since my phone's in my hand, and I'm blowing up Mandy's cell like nobody's business, gushing over the hot man and the hot mess he left me in, only pausing my gossip to apologize for being a selfish friend and ask if she made her flight.

About five minutes later, I get a series of messages:

Mandy: **Oh, wow.**

Mandy: **How embarrassing.**

Mandy: **Send me a pic.**

Mandy: **Yes, I made the flight, but I have a really bad seat.**

Me: **No way. I'm not snapping a photo. I'm embarrassed enough.**

Mandy: **Ask.**

Me: **Uh. No.**

Is this girl insane? It's rude to just snap pictures of people going about their business. I wouldn't like it one bit.

Mandy: **I need some eye candy for my flight.**

Me: **Stick some Skittles in your eyes.**

I roll my eyes and bob my head up, admiring his ears. Then harrumph at myself before typing away. *Who the hell finds ears attractive?*

Mandy: **You're no fun. I'm going to be bored af.**

Me: **Your flight is less than three hours. You will be out of that seat soon! Me, I'm stuck over here after making a total dork of myself.**

Mandy: **Just be direct 'Hey, I think you're totally hot. Can you take a picture with me?'**

Me: **Sure. I'll do that right after I ask the genie for a million dollars and for a magical bladder that empties on its own.**

Mandy: **Two million. That way we can share. And WTF?**

Me: **I have to pee, but I don't want to get up until we get in the air.**

Mandy: **Why? It's a perfect opportunity for you to get his picture and stir up conversation.**

Me: **I'd rather give you a million dollars than make a fool out of myself twice. Entertain yourself. I'm sure there are cute faces to ogle while you're flying in the air.**

Mandy: **I'm sitting between an elderly couple that keeps yelling at each other over me. They don't want to switch seats because they don't want to sit next to each other. They haven't even closed the aircraft door, and it already feels like a lifetime.**

I giggle. The flight attendant must have heard because she stops beside me. "Miss, we ask that all our passengers turn down their portable devices."

I thank her for reminding me. "Does this flight have Wi-Fi access?"

She replies, "I'm sorry, no."

Pretending to put the cell phone on airplane mode, I ask, "May I get a glass of water?"

As she leaves to get the drink, I text Mandy one more time.

Me: **Got caught. No Wi-Fi, signing out**.

I catch the last message just before putting away my phone.

Mandy: **Ahh! I am not going to make it.**

I sit back to relax as the flight attendant drops off a bottle of water. "Thank you." I check the time. Five hours left to go and nothing to do.

Oh no! Why did I give my backpack to Mr. 3B Hottie? My laptop and reader are both above his head. I can't ask him to get it down again; it's too embarrassing, and I'm too short to reach it on my own. At least not without standing on the edge of the chair and hanging on to the overhead to reach inside. I picture the movement in my head and decide against it. What if my bag hits him again?

These planes are not very accessible for short people. I'm not extremely short like some people at school might imply. I am almost 5'2" in high heels, which I am not wearing. They'd come in handy right about now.

To distract myself, I slump in my seat and flip through the movies on the monitor attached to Mr. 3B Hottie's seat, careful not to press too hard and attract more attention. Mortification is the ultimate level of embarrassment. I think catatonic state comes after.

Two for two. Settling on some sitcom I haven't watched in

a while, I press play and sip on my bottled water. Then I realize it's not going to help my overflowing bladder, so I cap it and store it in the seat pouch.

Mr. 3B Hottie shoots up from his seat, surprising me. I think he's going to say something, but he heads toward the front end of the plane.

Now is my chance. I'm out of my seat and standing on the edge of his in no time. With the overhead bin open, I curl my fingers around the ledge, anchoring myself, and reach in with my other hand, feeling around for the bag. I hook my fingers through the bag strap and pull it to the rim.

"I could have gotten that for you." His voice comes from nearby.

Startled, I lose my grip, flailing and searching for something to grab on to. I release my backpack, which falls, and unfortunately, I fall right behind it. Closing my eyes, I brace myself for the impact. Instead, I hear a thump, some rustling, and I am suddenly not falling but being held.

I slowly open one eye, then the other, staring at the top of the plane. I look to the ground and see I am hovering in the arms of Mr. 3B Hottie. Flexed muscles and a soft grin greet me.

A 'thank you' forms in the back of my throat but nothing comes out.

He keeps holding me, staring down at me, effortlessly keeping me up in the air. In a low voice, he says, "I'm sorry. I didn't mean to startle you. Are you okay?"

I nod, as I admire his chiseled face, warm eyes, firm lips—hmm, he is probably a great kisser.

"Can I put you down?" he asks.

I nod again. As he slowly lowers me, I grip on to the lapels of his blazer and wait until my feet hit the floor. Embarrassed, I attempt to step away but my body screams to stay near him. I force my feet to move, wobbling back a step.

Still very close to him, due to the small corridor of the plane, I can smell his cologne and feel his body heat. I avoid looking up into his earnest brown eyes and snap back to reality—the reality of how I got there into his arms. Replaying the preceding events forces them to sink in, and I don't even blush. At this point, nothing I can do will humiliate me any further. I just fell on the plane. In front of everyone, I could have hurt myself or someone else.

He bends down to pick up my backpack from the floor, rubbing the back of his head.

"Oh no." I hurt him again. The crushing realization that my bag just fell on top of the most gorgeous man on earth for a second time, banishes my previous notion. And I turn crimson—scarlet red, like a lobster. I'm broken. I have achieved a new level of embarrassment, and it's called the living dead.

"Here you go," he says as he passes me my bag.

I'm breathing and functioning on the inside, but my lips aren't moving. He probably thinks I'm mute.

Worried, he asks again, "Are you sure you are okay?"

Since words have evaded me and my voice box has nailed itself shut, I salute him, like an idiot, and smile. The nod that comes after answers his question, and I aim for my seat to show I'm okay. I must be a little wobbly because he holds on to my arm and helps me sit down.

Touching. Doesn't. Help. Each word floats up to my brain like a firework, sending little warm flecks of heat all over my mind. I'm tingling, and I haven't even said a word.

"Can I get you something?"

I look up at him again and notice a small scratch at the side of his face. Without a second thought, my hand goes to his forehead. "I hurt you, I'm so sorry," I whisper.

He beams at my response. "I'm okay. Are you? You had me worried there for a bit."

I smile back. "Yes, just shaken I think."

He points to his seat. "I am right here if you need me. Just let me know." He waits for me to bob my head in agreement, canting his lips as if amused by my reaction.

"Thanks." The words slip out just as the flight attendant comes to us. After noticing all the commotion, she jokingly asks, "Are paramedics required?"

"We are both good." He chuckles and glances down at me. "No paramedics needed."

Just a defibrillator. Good God that smile can stop a woman's heart.

CHAPTER TWO

Genie

MINA

I made it through the rest of the flight without any more tragic memories that will cause me sleepless nights. As I save my research paper and close the laptop, I smile contentedly. No more trips, falls, or knocking people on the head with items. At least not yet.

After stuffing my laptop in my backpack, I glance up at Mr. 3B Hottie, who is smiling down at me with my carry-on already in his hands. A tickling sensation consumes the pit of my stomach, spreading warmth from head to toe.

I smile back. "Thanks."

His hand lingers on the handle as I grab it. "How are you doing?"

"I'm okay." In reality I can't stop thinking how cozy his hand feels next to mine—how I want that warmth nearer. "And you?" I ask, gesturing to the scratch on his head.

"I am not as banged up as I look." He winks, releasing the handle of my bag.

We both exit the plane behind one another. I, of course, admire his physique as I follow. Nice, muscular, and strong stride. I look down as he steps to the side and lets me pass in front of him, once again catching me admiring him. A flush of heat floods my face.

I smile up at him. "Thank you," I whisper as I pass just inches from him. *I keep walking away from his warmth.*

Before I change my mind and go back to Mr. 3B Hottie and kiss him, I speed walk to the baggage claim area without looking back. An incredible urge to run back to his arms takes over my thoughts. I bypass everything and straight-line to the coffee stand. *Caffeine will help get my mind off of him.* After ordering, I wait for my mocha Frappuccino while ordering a ride to pick me up. It's about ten minutes away, just enough time to vlog.

I tap on the record button. "Hi, everyone! Shout out to all my followers with a flying phobia, I made it! I had a rocky start, almost missed my flight, but all is well now. As you can probably see from the background, it's a full airport. Tons of people, and they will all be rushing to get their ride soon. So I have to say goodbye to beat the traffic." I wiggle my fingers in the air, waving goodbye, and end the live, just as the barista calls my name.

I take my drink to go and head out to the New York streets. I have been commuting to New York since Mom divorced my dad. I wasn't even thirteen when it happened. I came back from boarding school for spring break to a lot of excessively loud discussions. Since then, holidays and breaks are difficult.

Freedom is nice. Had I stayed here instead of going to California for school, my father would have sheltered me my whole life, and I'd be dealing with my mother's overbearing attitude. *Is it too late to go back to school?*

During the car ride to Mom's, I pause to check the phone. Lots of messages about what happened on the video and Mandy sent a text: **Your video has gone viral!**

OMG! I have to see. Do I have poop on my face or something? Embarrassment gone viral. Can it be worse than what happened on the plane?

I rewatch my livestream. I look fine, no boogers, thank God. As I continue watching, I can't understand why it went viral. I read a few more comments and take another look at the video. In the background, I see an older man falling on the escalator while another man catches him midway. At the bottom of the escalator, he helped the older man off, and they spoke for a few minutes. Then the hero turned toward the camera as he walked away.

That's him! I respond to the flooding comments. **That's Mr. 3B Hottie. He is the one that caught me when I was falling on the plane.**

I text Mandy a screenshot of my video.

Me: **There is your picture. Sorry it's blurry. I wish I wasn't such a spaz. He gave me all the fuzzy feelings.**

Mandy: **Way ahead of you. Check out the link I sent you.**

Mandy had already reposted a comment with a close-up of Mr. 3B Hottie, playing the matchmaker. The sight of him causes me to smile, but it's quickly replaced with a frown when I read her message. "Mr. 3B Hottie. Hero of the day. If you know more info. Please let me know."

I see right through this, she's trying to chance a meeting, but the chances of him seeing this are basically nonexistent. But if she wants to be my ring genie, and use the Internet to grant my wishes, then by all means, let me rub away.

I post my story: **Mr. 3B Hottie is the gentleman who saved me from a bad fall on the plane. All I know about him is his seat number, that he is handsome with an incredible smile and warm eyes. If you see this, thank you for your help.**

***

A couple weeks later I walk into my dorm room, abandon my bag at the door, and hop on my bed, completely exhausted from winter break and so happy to be back in the calm of things.

"Hi, Mina." Mandy enters my room right after me.

"I need a nap." I bury my face into the comfy pillow. I've been talking to people every day; I just need a day to be alone.

"How was your vacation?"

I flip my head to the side and peek at her. "What vacation? I had to cancel the trip."

She looks as offended as I feel. "What?"

"My mom forced me to stay home for a family gathering. Which turned into an announcement about her engagement, and a meet and greet of the family-to-be."

"You didn't tell me any of that. You said it was boring, and then you ghosted me. I got no response until today. I thought you met someone and I would never see you again. I was planning on calling the police if you didn't turn up today."

She's exaggerating but it makes me smile.

I sit up, slumping against the wall. "It was horrible, and I didn't want to ruin your vacation by spending hours complaining, not that I had a minute to myself."

"Mina, how bad could it have been?" Mandy asks as she sits down on the bed next to me and crosses her legs.

"After my mother's boyfriend popped the question, my real vacation was canceled and the remainder of the vacation turned into wedding plans. I hate frilly pink crap."

"No Mexico?" Mandy asks. "No tequila?"

I smirk when she elbows me and shake my head, slightly banging it on the wall. "It didn't happen. It took two weeks to set up a place for the wedding, a time and date, and getting a wedding dress, flowers, and catering ideas. Apparently, it takes two years to prepare for a wedding."

Mandy opens her mouth to ask a question, but I hold up my finger for her to wait.

"My mom does not want to wait that long. So, there was a lot of drama, pleading, and bribery going on for my mother to get her spring wedding, when and where she wanted it. The bridal gown has been picked and the order rushed. At this rate, this wedding is going to cost ten times more than all our years of college put together." I roll my eyes and crack the tense bones in my neck. "You should see the invitations. Beautiful, but super expensive."

Mandy giggles. "Is she marrying King Tut or something?"

"Wealthier, according to his son."

"By the way, you and your family are invited. My mom is going to call you later for your address and your parents' address."

"Call, why? I can text her the address, or you can."

"She insists."

She shrugs. "Why are you still frowning? You are here, and your mom will handle the rest, right? You're free from matrimonial hell until spring."

My face must truly have a bad expression. She talks slower, then stops. "Aren't you?"

"Not really," I answer. "I have to come up with choices for flowers and bridesmaid dresses this week. She gave me homework on my vacation." I reluctantly get up and grab the small bag out of my suitcase, and empty it onto the mattress. It's filled with wedding things and a few magazines. "Will you help me? I know nothing about weddings."

"Me neither," Mandy replies, picking up and reading the titles of each. "I'm going to grab my laptop. We need more than magazines to get this right."

"True," I say. "I will grab my planner and a notepad."

She pops out of the room and returns with the cord and the laptop and plugs it in. "Before we get started, tell me more about this new future brother of yours. Any chance of me becoming your sister-in-law?"

Eww. "Maybe it's better to get my new stepfather and Mom to adopt you."

She chuckles as she lifts the top of her computer and rubs her hands together.

CHAPTER THREE

Forced Vacation

Dean

After being summoned in person by his receptionist, I knock on the wooden door of John's office. "Hello, boss. You wanted to see me?"

It must be important. I can't remember the last time I was called in here.

John purses his lips and folds his hands on the table, waiting until I'm further inside before telling me, "Have a seat."

As I sit down, he stands and ambles over to the door to advise the receptionist, "Can you hold my calls and get the tech in here?"

Tech? I chuckle, thinking he's jostling me. I submitted all my paperwork from the flight, and I hate the Internet, so I'm not wasting my time flirting with some chick for accounting through company mail or searching for things I shouldn't be searching for during office hours. "What's this all about, John?"

Turning to me, he closes the door. "Dean." The pause advises me this is serious. "I know it's been a long time since you've been hired, but I have to ask: do you remember the rules about social media and the Internet?"

"Of course I remember, John. It's not like someone can forget something like that. The company sends out yearly training on it, reminding people the different ways that social media can cause problems, place our families and all the people we protect in danger."

"Yes. Because of this, anyone caught using social media is subject to job loss." John walks over to me and leans against the desk.

"I don't understand. Is there a training module I missed?"

John doesn't say a thing for a few minutes while I wait impatiently trying to figure it out.

"Theo's coming in to help me out with this. I know nothing about these posters, frogs, and Tweety birds."

I glance behind him to his older computer. It is currently being used to hold up files and stacks of papers, the keyboard is his paperweight keeping it all in place.

"Well, do you have anything to say for yourself?"

I look back and shrug. "I, ummm, I'm not sure, but I think Tweety bird was a cartoon from my childhood."

A knock saves me from the awkward moment. Theo walks in with a laptop in his hand.

John straightens himself and gestures to the extra seat near the coat rack. "Pull up a chair and join us."

After Theo brings over a chair, I get up and shake Theo's hand, then we both settle into our chairs.

John remains standing in front of us so he can see what Theo is typing. "Can you please tell Dean about the things you told me about and how it caught a virus?"

Theo glances between us and decides not to correct his error, but instead lifts a finger in the air. "I have a better idea. I can show him." Theo lifts the laptop to demonstrate he is prepared.

John nods his agreement, and I'm stuck with a stupefied look on my face. "What are you two going on about?" I've worked with John for years. We get along, and he's usually honest with me, so why are we beating around the bush?

Theo lowers his gaze and strike enter on the keyboard before swiveling the screen toward me. The video portrays me saving an old man from toppling over on the stairs.

"I-I-uh..." I begin to stutter, "I don't understand. I'm in here because I saved a guy and someone caught me on video?" That doesn't exactly give my job away.

"No, not quite," John refutes and points to the screen.

"You are here because this video went viral," Theo adds.

"I didn't post it." I shake my head. This was weeks ago. "I didn't put that on the Internet or make it go viral. So why am I here? How is it affecting my job? Besides, tomorrow some dog will play a piano and no one will remember this video."

Theo clucks his tongue and hisses before scrolling down. "Well... It's been weeks and it keeps increasing in popularity."

I shake my head, not fully comprehending what is happening. "What do you mean?"

John asks in an accusatory manner, "Was it you who saved the old man?"

"Of course, I did, but there is no law in saving people from injury."

"No," John answers. "But tons of people are commenting about your identity. And you're being searched for."

"Searched?" I face Theo, asking for a clarification.

Theo shows me a different video of myself. I'm mesmerized as I watch myself at a supermarket parking lot, and throw my head back. I quickly remember what had happened. I saw a runaway cart with a cute little baby girl, the mom noticed too late. She threw the grocery bags on the floor and tried to run to get her baby heading into the lot traffic.

"You can't really tell who it is stopping the cart." But whoever had been filming got closer when I returned the baby and cart back to the mother. With a smile, I nodded to the mom as she thanked me, then waved goodbye to the little one.

"That's definitely you," John almost shouts.

I nod, knowing he won't want to hear any excuse. It's not like I could wish for a new face.

John points to Theo, and there is another video. *It's me again.* This meeting is getting worse. I can barely look at the screen.

"Theo says that's you too," John's voice catches my attention.

I jump out of my seat, pacing. "It's me but I didn't put any of those videos on the Internet." I didn't breach the company rules.

John sympathizes with me, but crosses his arms. "No, you didn't. But going viral is bringing unnecessary attention, and when people see you, they are going to be looking for you. It's only a matter of time before they figure out what you do for a living and put your life at risk."

Theo says something, but all I can do is organize my thoughts.

I cut Theo off mid-sentence, "But, it's someone else who put the video online. It's not right I get penalized for something I didn't do." I curl my fingers around the chair. "Just ask Theo; he has been to my house. I don't own a computer. I had one social media account in college. Everyone had Messenger to call with, but I haven't used any of that since I came to work here. Besides these things are temporary, and they don't even know who I am." I take my seat. "So no harm done."

Theo is smiling. "They named you."

"Named me?" *Everyone knows I don't want to be known on social media.*

Theo clears his throat. "You are currently known as Mr. 3B Hottie."

John coughs; I think he is trying to fight off laughter. There is even a tear in his eye from strain.

"I understand," I say after my jaw goes back to its place. "You guys are joking with me, right? How did you get all those videos?"

John and Theo look at each other for a couple seconds, as if communicating through just eye contact. They simultaneously look back at me.

Theo softly says, "This isn't a joke. We didn't film you; someone else did. Look." He gestures to the person who posted the latest video. "This is the origin."

John says, "Someone thinks you are really good-looking." He chokes back another cough. "But according to the comments, they are reporting sightings. The mom of the kid from the cart even said her hometown. This is serious."

"I can see how this can be an issue. Can't the tech nerds erase them or something?" I plead.

"I resent that. We are more than just tech nerds. And we tried, but as soon as we managed to take some down another one came up and the cycle repeated itself," Theo starts the sentence with such confidence, but by the end he was basically mumbling.

The inevitable consumes my thoughts, and I gather what is left of my ego. "So the solution is to fire me?"

"Not fired," John explains. "Just on a very long vacation to see if we can get this handled."

"Or until you get ugly," Theo jokes. "No one would be looking for Mr. 3B Ugly." He snorts at himself, mumbling, "It'd be more like Mr. 3 C-U-L8tr."

"I don't know what you are talking about," I shoot back before addressing my boss. He knows me, he's been like my uncle in the workplace. "What 'if' we can't handle things?" I growl out in a slightly passive aggressive tone.

"We will revisit it then. Meanwhile, your vacation starts tomorrow. Enjoy and stay out of the limelight," he warns in a kind tone as he opens the door.

CHAPTER FOUR

Band of Friends

Dean

A week into my forced vacation and still no improvements on the work front. If anything, Theo says it's getting worse. Another story came out about me. Random people posting about meeting me or someone who looks like me. At least this person said I was in London. They are calling me the Nameless Prince and speculating on who I am. I even saw some woman offer an IPad to whoever could find me and another one offered her panties.

It's annoying, and I've been keeping myself out of the prying eye. The last thing I need is someone I know identifying me online. But, I'm going stir crazy.

I'm sitting on my couch, contemplating heating up the lasagna Mom brought over and flipping through TV channels when Theo calls to check in on me. I think about how losing my job will affect her. It's just been the two of us since Dad died, and then I met John, who helped me get where I am.

Unfortunately, it ends with me on the couch moping around. It's been a week since I've hung out with my friends, and I'm tired of being locked up, so I call the boys over to the house for some beers and poker night with an ulterior motive.

The five of us have always been there for each other since we were kids, and I think together we can figure something out.

Ralph's the first to arrive, since he lives close by. He doesn't even have to knock since he has the extra key to my house. "Yo, brother." He stretches one arm out and hooks me into a hug, tapping my back twice before releasing me. "Glad you called." He balances the bowl of dip on the other hand.

"Thanks for coming over." I nod and lead him into the kitchen, grabbing us two beers with pop-off caps. He is the first friend I ever made and one of the one's who'd drop anything to help me out. Growing up as only children with moms who struggled to get by bound us.

"I was in the mood for some poker, so I called the guys over."

"Cool..." He spots the lasagna in the fridge when he adds the bowl in and yanks it out. Making himself at home, he grabs a fork and digs in, moaning at the goodness. "Your mom can cook. Wish she gave my mom some lessons." He pops a huge square of pasta layers in his mouth. "Your mom spoils you with all the good food."

I laugh as he devours the home-cooked meal. "She always makes extra because she knows you'll stop in." He's a money geek who likes to cook, but the man can eat and Mom always says food is the glue of families and friendships.

I sip on my beer when the doorbell rings. "The States are here…" Ralph predicts.

"How do you know it's them and not Theo?"

"Theo's always late." He takes another chunk before hiding the lasagna back in the fridge and checking on his dip. He winks at me and pulls it out. "Better answer the door and let them in before I lick this and claim it as mine."

I warn him not to with a quick scowl and head for the door through the short hallway. Hernand and Robert State are twin brothers, who joined our group in high school.

We get to talking, ordering food and watching Sports-Center while waiting for Theo. By the time he arrives, we're in front of a blaring TV with beer and an open pizza box on the coffee table.

A loud cheer goes out when he comes into the living room with a messenger bag around his neck.

"I take it that cheer is not for my arrival," Theo asks. "I have difficulty believing you guys are that happy to see me."

"*Manito*, you know we love you." Hernando points to the box of beer in Theo's hand. "The booze man always gets the bear hugs."

Robert State, the largest of the two brothers and the more silent one, stands beside Theo's thin frame, threatening him with an embrace. "You brought the good stuff."

Theo's not a hugger, but he fist bumps the man and pats him on the back before handing the box to Robert. "Put those muscles to work and distribute."

A round of half-hugs, handshakes, and hellos go around. I grab some beer from the fridge and urge Theo to join in. I wait until he's put a slice or two in his stomach and for the commercials to come on before bringing it up.

"Theo…" I nod upward. "How are things at work? John's screening my calls."

"Dude, you're nearly stalking him. Can you blame the man?"

"Yes," I answer adamantly and place the empty beer bottle on the floor. "Does it look—am I getting fired?"

All of them stop in their tracks and wait for me to explain, but I don't. Theo takes over the explanation stuff for me when Ralphs asks, "What did you do?"

"Nothing," I clarify, explanations are not my strong suit.

Theo responds, "He has gone viral."

Everyone chuckles and a few remarks follow. I don't really know who they belong to because I only catch a few since they are talking over each other.

"No way, this man is living in the past."

"He's still rocking a flip phone."

"He doesn't own a computer."

"He's the oldest young dude we know."

Lots of chuckles at my cost come, and I let them have their fun. Because they are all true. The guy who hates the Internet, avoids it like the plague, has gone Internet Famous.

"Believe it." I tell all of them as I reach into the box of beer, that's surprisingly cold, and twist it open.

"Yeah." Theo nods as he wipes his hands on a napkin.

Thankfully, not my carpet or Mom would bite my head off on her next visit. She likes for me to keep a tidy home, and when I don't, I feel like a tiny boy again, getting berated for not following the rules.

"Search it up." Theo points to his phone and gives it to Ralph, who looks at me with a worried look on his face. He knows how much this must be affecting me. "Type in 'Mr. 3B

Hottie. It's gotten so bad, he's been on the news in a few states."

There is a roar of laughter at the new label.

"Who is calling you hot?" Ralphs says sarcastically to lighten the mood and grabs one of the empty dip bowls with remnants of his famous fire-alarm jalapeno dip from the coffee table. "This is way hotter than you."

"Funny." I roll my eyes at his joke, grateful for it though. "But this isn't a joke. I'm going to get fired."

Theo intervenes. "No one said you're going to get fired."

Ralph pops his shoulder. "He's got a point. This stuff fades fast. You just have to ride it out and hang low."

The brothers look at each other and simultaneously join in, "Bro Time."

I'm counting on it. "They wouldn't force me into vacation for just a weak fad," I say. "It's got to be more serious."

At the severity in my tone, everyone grabs their cells at the same time to check.

"I don't have Wi-Fi," I remind the geeks who can't live a day without touching their phones. Hell, a couple hours is a lot.

"Come, I will show you." Theo grabs his laptop from its case, and we all head into the kitchen for supplies. It's also where Theo gets the best signal. He plugs in his wireless router near the coffee machine and sets up his computer on the island.

As the guys see the first video, Hernand is the first to comment. "*Manito*, check out all these views. You famous." He whoops his hands in there, getting laughs from the others.

His brother chimes in. "Mr. Hot Stuff."

Theo corrects him. "No. Mr. 3B Hottie."

They enjoy making me squirm and whistling.

Hernando squeezes my bicep, checking out my muscles. Giving in to the laughter and whistles, I stop and flex my pecs, first right pose then change to the left. I subtly hold both arms forward, and my middle fingers slowly raise upward.

"Oh, check it out. The boy's got moves," Robert jokes.

"I got some moves you haven't seen yet," I say in a serious voice, taking some steps toward them.

"Save that for your mystery woman, Mr. 3B," Ralph pipes up as he refills the small bowls of dip from the master supply.

Another roar of laughter goes out.

Theo stands up from the stool next to me. "You guys should have recorded his performance just now. It would probably have gone around the world in less than an hour."

Ralph calms everyone down by asking the serious question. "Dude, what are you going to do?"

I shrug. "I know nothing about this stuff, that's why I called you guys. I can use all the help I can get because I can't lose my job. I love being an air marshal, and John said I was well on my way up the ranks. I wouldn't know what else to do?"

Theo relaxes his arms around my shoulders. "I mean... you could always model."

I scowl at him, and he throws his hands up in defense.

Ralph chimes in, "I could tell you if those numbers were dollars instead of views you wouldn't have to worry about working anymore. But, since it isn't and your job has stern rules on this, you're screwed."

Hernand offers, "You can always come work with the two of us. You would fit right in at the security company." They asked me to join the day they started it. I was in flight school then and John was helping me out.

"Thanks for the offer. With the way things are going, I might be in need of it," I reply, "but for now, I should do everything I can to keep this one. So gang, does anyone have any solution?"

Hernarnd faces Theo as he loads a chip with dip. "Theo, are you sure there is nothing else you can do on that computer to get rid of this problem?"

Theo replies, "It's not a magic lamp, you know? It's not like you can rub it and make a wish and poof problem solved. It's a computer, and there is only so much it can do."

"Then what can you do?" Ralph looks over at me and hooks his arm on his neck, waiting for an answer. "Can you figure out who posted it?"

Theo cocks his head to the side. "That I know."

The whole room halts to look at him, but I'm the one who opens my arms to the air, asking for more information with a flabbergasted harrumph. "Why didn't you tell me?"

"Does it matter?" Theo types away on the keyboard. "Even if she takes it down, other people will keep posting stuff about you."

Ralph walks over to stand behind Theo and watch the screen while I grab myself another beer, succumbing to the idea of being fired. Either I wait it out or I wait it out. My options are reduced to one, and that really doesn't sit well with me.

It's the burly State brother who breaks through the tense room, "Look!" He holds his phone out. "What if you meet up with her? Ask her to take it down and say she found you. Then all of this will die down and people won't be curious."

"Or," Ralph answers. "It'll get worse."

"Worse, how?" I ask, shutting the fridge. "I'm stuck inside my house, living like a recluse, while watching my career—one I've worked very hard for—disintegrate in front of me. Don't know what you guys are thinking, but famous people don't do well in blending in." I point toward the brothers and shrug. "Honestly, this is the only other option next to waiting, right?"

"It's not a bad idea." Theo swivels on the stool to face the guys. "We can find out a little bit about her."

Hernand shrugs and bobs his head. "We can look into it."

"No, I don't want to dig into her personal life or invade her privacy."

"Why not?" Ralph taps on the touch screen, like he's magnifying an image. "What kind of privacy do you have? She straight out blew your life up." Ralph turns the screen around to show me the beautiful girl who popularized me. "Mina the Bloggerina."

I scoff at the picture of the little miss who fell into my arms. Her reddish brown curly hair, her soft brown eyes, her voluptuous curves... I gently stroke the side of my face where her bag had scratched me and can't help but feel a tinge of excitement flood through me. Had I not been working that flight, I would have introduced myself, maybe even asked her for a coffee and a number. She is so incredibly beautiful, and for a second when our eyes connected and her tongue darted over her bottom lip, I almost forgot that I didn't flirt during work hours, but it was so damn difficult to put her down and not kiss her.

Ralph bumps my shoulder. "She's cute. Do you know her?"

Rubbing my forehead and casting the thoughts away, I

answer. "Sort of. She's this short girl who couldn't reach the overhead bin, and she was blocking my view of the captain's door."

"Blocking or distracting?" Robert asks, as he scrolls through her blog looking at flat-lays of her desk station and pictures of her. He stops at a picture of her on the beach in a one-piece that is way hotter than any bikini I've seen. "I'd be a whole lot distracted if she showed up in front of me. Damn, now that's what I call some dangerous curves."

I was both. I clench my jaw at the guys gawking at her, but because I have no stake over her and didn't even know her name until today, I simmer down. "When the flight attendant called me up for an update, Mina the Bloggerina got up to grab her backpack." I remember the way she looked at me and her shyness and chuckle. "She was a mess, and I caught her before she fell on the customers."

"See that's where you go wrong." Theo dabs his finger against his temple. "Thinking like a hero always screws you over."

Ralph smacks Theo's hand down. "Shut up. Like you wouldn't do the same."

A scowling Theo gets up from his chair. "If she looked like that, hell yeah, but I mean, Dean always has to play the hero."

"It's my job. To avoid people dying and getting hurt."

"Your job is to maintain safety in the clouds, not help people down here on earth. You do this stuff because you think that's what your father would do."

He's not wrong. Dad died a hero, but that's not why I do it.

"That doesn't matter." Ralph sighs and intrudes on my thoughts. "She lives in California."

"How do you know that?" Hernand comes to Ralph's side, followed by his brother. Now all three of them crowd the island. "Look, see these photos? The emblem on the notebooks. Sharyar University."

Hernand isn't impressed. "It could just be because the colors match and stuff."

"No," Robert corrects and shows a few photos. "She's wearing a few hoodies from them, and the T-shirt here has the King mascot. You don't own that many school insignia things unless you go there."

"Go there..." Hernand nods at me. "Locate her and see where it goes."

CHAPTER FIVE

Sultan's Palace

DEAN

The next day, Theo, Ralph, and I land in a private airport after flying on a private plane to California, thanks to the State brothers who hooked us up. They called in a favor with one of their security clients so I didn't have to risk getting identified. The second we hit the street though, I'm astutely aware of all the people looking at us.

"This wasn't such a great idea," I say as we get in the rental car waiting for us on the curb.

"Well, we ain't bad to look at." Ralph shrugs it off as he gets in the driver's side door and enters the pin into the compartment to get the keys and the rental papers. Then pops the trunk for us while he confirms with the company on the phone.

Theo and I plop our bags in. Mostly, I shield my face until

Theo points out none of the pedestrians have phones pointed in our direction, which eases my nerves.

"So what's our first move?" he asks, shutting the hood. Before we got on the plane, the brothers told us Sharyar University was a closed campus. Privately owned and only students and people with visitors passes got in.

"I have no idea. Check into the hotel. Where's it at?"

"About twenty minutes from here." Theo had picked a hotel nearest to the location of her last post. She had checked in at a bistro that was also in the university's vicinity. "I'm starving though." He checks his watch as he rounds the car and takes the navigator seat. "It's getting late. Maybe we can grab some dinner near campus. With some luck, she'll be around."

I climb into the backseat, noting Ralph had gotten off the call. "San Diego is huge. Guessing where she's going to be will take forever. We need to get into the university. Can't the State brothers get us some visitors passes?"

"They tried," Ralph says as he hits the fob's power button. The engine roars to life. "They said no one got back to them. Something about burning bridges with some chick."

Theo locks his seatbelt into place, and I do the same. "I've been following her online. Her last post was in a coffee shop near the hotel, and before that at a shopping mall. So, I think she sticks around here."

Stalking isn't usually the way I meet women, but desperate times, call for different measures. "So, we search around this location until she posts something new?"

Theo brings his phone up and shows a map with a bunch of pinned locations in different color balloons. "Reds are the ones she goes to more than three times in the last year. Yellow two times. Green once."

"And the blue?" I reach forward to enlarge his screen.

"Our first stop tonight. A local lounge club. She goes there often, so who knows, maybe your girl will show up."

"Not my girl," I correct. "We barely talked."

"You don't have to talk to—"

Ralph cuts Theo off. "We need to get a few drinks in Dean first. Try to shake off the cop look. He is so stiff, he is liable to scare the girl away."

Theo replies, "Well, don't loosen him up too much you know, his girl might wind up liking him stiff."

"I don't look like a cop."

"See what I mean?" Ralph says to Theo. "You make a crack on his anatomy, and he is worried about looking like a cop."

Theo says, "It's a good thing he brought us with him. He would be like a lost puppy."

Ralph glances back at me, taking his eyes off the road for a few seconds. "When was the last time you went out and just relaxed or gone bar hopping?"

"Four nights after he graduated college," Theo jokes. "Or was it three before you decided that serious is the only way to go?"

I open my mouth to contradict what they are saying, but they're right. That's when my mom needed my help the most. She started to have problems standing on her feet and had a minor heart attack. My days of living the life came to an end. I didn't want to lose her, so I told her I'd take care of her. Also, I would not have made it this far without them, and I don't go bar hopping. I've been all about work and saving money for the better part of my adulthood.

I reply anyways, "In the first place, I would not look like a lost puppy, since I'm smart enough not to come alone and bring my friends. Secondly, I hear women like lost puppies. They find them irresistible."

"You're right," Ralph says. "I have been going fishing with the wrong bait all this time. Maybe I should take pointers from you."

Theo sways his head from side to side, tucking his phone into his front jacket pocket. "Only if you want to end up dateless and alone."

"Hey! I go on dates."

"Taking your mom to the Golden Plate doesn't count as a date," Theo jibes. "It's sweet though, but we're talking real girls."

"Screw you guys." I sit back and glance out the window, thinking about the last few years of my life. I can't even remember the last time I had a girlfriend. Between work and —well, work—I don't get much free time. I'm always traveling and on layovers, or at the gym training. When I get a minute, I like to check in with Mom, and having a steady girlfriend who understands my job and obligations is hard to come by.

"This place is too crowded." We weave our way through the crowd at Sultan's Palace, looking for the bar. There's a lot of seated areas with cushions and sheer curtains, and is that a bong-shaped lamp? "What the hell is this place?"

Theo ignores my question while Ralph is too far ahead to hear it.

When we come to one of the three long bars, we gather around each other.

"How are we ever going to find her here?" I ask as Theo tries to flag down the bartender who is dressed like a genie.

Ralph puts his hand on my shoulder. "We never knew if this would work anyway. All we can do is wait and see if she posts something."

Theo angles his body toward us, resting his lean elbow on the bar top. "We can split up and see if we see her. She may not post that she's here."

I nod as the bartender places three beers in front of Theo. "Do you still have her picture?"

Ralph pays for the drinks and tips the pretty bartender while Theo digs into his pocket to get his phone. He shoots us all the picture through text.

After distributing the beers, Ralph gets a good look at the picture and whistles. "Still fine."

I don't need to check my phone. I still remember what she looks like. It's been hard not to think about her and hate her a little bit at the same time. If she hadn't caught me, then I would be living my life like usual rather than chasing her down on the opposite coast. "She's short," I tell the guys as I measure the air and stop around my chest. "Like five-five, if that, with heels."

Ralph salutes me and disappears to the left, up the stairs that have an open balcony and booths. "It kind of looks like the Taj Mahal in here."

Theo sips his beer and points to the right. "I'm kind of

liking this place. Music, chill, and those pillows offer optimal hook-up spots... That's where I'm going."

"We're here to find the girl," I shout over the music.

"Meet you at the bar in an hour," Theo says as he blends in with the dancing crowd. Within seconds I get a group text from Ralph insisting we text if we find her. Since no one comes to a place like this without drinking, I saunter over to the middle bar with the stools and wait for an empty one. After taking a seat, I swing the cushion around to face the crowd. It provides the optimal view of both bars. I focus my eyesight on the shorter girls with matching hair, but none of them are as beautiful as Mina.

After about half an hour of scanning and wasting way too much on beer, I yank out my phone and type in her website. Her social media handles are in the upper bar, and I click on one, which links me to a public feed. Tons of video blogs about planners, study guides, travel, and wedding planning.

Crap. What if she's getting married or something? I ask myself, only to realize that I'm here to get her to help me, not to date the girl.

It works for all of a minute before I pull up the video and check the post date. *Not that long ago.*

That sends me down a whole new path where I play the videos I can't hear to check for a ring, which luckily, she doesn't have. I'm not sure why that makes me smile, but there's also no guy in any of her recent pictures. *Maybe she's as single as I am.*

The phone buzzes in my hand, distracting me. A message in our group chat from Theo, which I echo back aloud, "She's coming here."

I sit up straighter, hoping to catch a glimpse of her

walking through the door. But I see lots of girls, none of them the treasure I seek.

Someone taps me on my shoulder, and I swivel around to find a pretty girl in a red shirt with frilly things on the hem and tight leather jeans that don't look like they come off. She flashes me her white smile, rimmed by velvety red lips.

"Do we know each other?" she asks, wedging herself between my barstool and the neighboring one. The guy on the other side doesn't seem to mind her butt touching his thigh. "You look familiar."

"Just visiting," I clip and flag the genie-tender, that's what they're called here, and wiggle my beer to get a refill.

"You waiting for someone?" she asks, obviously not making a move to leave.

"Yeah. I'm here with some friends." When a guy doesn't ask questions or look at a girl, it usually means he's not interested. She doesn't get the hint to leave and she keeps staring at me, which I don't like.

"I know where I know you from. Mr. 3B Hottie, right?"

"Who?" I contort my face in disgust, playing dumb.

"From the Internet." She blushes and tugs her phone out, searching for something on it, but luckily, doesn't point it at me. "Oh, I can't find it now. But there's some posts about some hero guy and I swear you look like him."

I hold my beer in the air and point to the three other bottles waiting on the counter. "Not a hero. Just a guy, trying to get over being dumped three hours ago." I lie but it does the trick.

Immediately, she feels bad. "Oh. That's awful."

"No offense, but I kind of just want to be alone. I was going to propose and it's been a shitty day."

Because she didn't come over to be my psychologist, she nods and walks away, tucking her phone into the very tight back pocket of her pants. Within seconds, she gets swooped up by some guy who takes her onto the dance floor and forgets about me. Or at least I hope she does.

Theo pops in with a girl in tow, then heads to the dance floor with the excuse that Mina may be on the dance floor. I highly doubt it.

Another hour goes by and nothing, no luck. I am losing hope blogger girl is even here at all, and I'm ready to go. When Theo returns without the arm candy, he's sweaty and three sips away from being intolerable. Mina or not, it's time we call it a night. Either she's here and we can't see her, or she didn't show up.

"Starting at a club wasn't the smartest idea," Theo surmises as he wipes the sweat off his forehead with a paper napkin.

"So was wearing a sweater." Ralph, who has been seated next to me, aiding me in my newest hobby—stalking—curls his finger under the collar to let air in. He's been complaining about the warmness here since he sat down.

"It's like looking for a needle in a haystack. I have been approached twice, as Mr. 3B Hottie." Ralph warded off the second one. "Luckily, no one took a picture of me."

Theo's face lights up and he snatches my arm, stopping the drink from reaching my lips. "That's brilliant."

"Your forehead?" Theo guffaws, handing him a clean napkin.

Theo takes it and wipes, clarifying what he meant in the process. "I can put out a post of you sighted at some place like the coffee shop. This way, they can come to us."

"Yah, I don't think so," I reply. "It's risky, and it would get both of us in hot water with John."

"Why don't you just email the blog?" Ralph adds, sliding off his chair.

"I did that." Theo seems annoyed at the question. "The email isn't working. She might have forgotten to change it to the new address." Theo tosses his sweaty napkin onto the counter and crooks his neck at us. "Let's go. I'm beat."

As soon as we hit the outside and fresh air fills our nostrils, Ralph points to the car. "So what do we do tomorrow? The girl's probably in class during the day."

Theo points to a billboard across the street, near where we parked the car. "How about the expo?"

CHAPTER SIX

Heaven in a Scone

Mina

"Mandy?" I yell from the corridor while knocking. "Are you ready?" This shouting is not a norm for me. I prefer Zen spaces but I'm running out of options. I have been texting and calling for twenty minutes with no answers, and our appointment is thirty minutes from now. "Hello?"

Mandy finally opens the door still in pajamas. "Morning." She waves to me and then swings the door back and aims straight for the bed to slide her slippers from underneath. She walks around the room, looking for something, not at all caring that we are running late. This is so unlike her.

"What are you doing? Mandy, we are running out of time. We have to be there soon."

She throws her head back and lifts a finger up in the air, gesturing for me to wait. "Coffee." She points to the pot, then walks into the bathroom. Hopefully, to wake herself up.

I walk over to the Keurig, pop in a K-cup, and brew her some caffeine. Then, look in the fridge for milk or cream.

Mandy comes out wearing normal clothes. Her shirt is perfectly ironed, but her face looks paler than usual. "Black is good." She slips the mug out and sips the steaming liquid without even flinching. "I'm ready to go."

I smile and shut the fridge. "Mandy, I have heard rumors of bed head being in again, but are you sure you want to test it out?"

She walks over to the mirror on the back side of her door and rolls her head in my direction. "It's not that bad."

"It's a mess." I take her coffee from her.

"Fine." She pops out a hair tie and puts her hair in a tight bun. "Okay, now I'm ready." She takes back her coffee. "Let's do this... By the way, when I said yes to being a bridesmaid at your mother's wedding, she never mentioned waking up at the ungodly hour of seven a.m. If this happens again, I will be very tempted to change my mind."

"I know the feeling. I can't believe how difficult it was to get up one hour earlier." I check my purse for my phone and the planner, then point to the door. "You got everything?"

"You wake up at eight? Are you crazy? That's too early." She checks herself in the mirror and swipes her makeup bag from the top of her dresser, then grabs her handbag.

"I don't want to," I point out. "I have Dr. P's classes at nine."

"Why didn't you take a later one?"

"He only teaches early morning classes." We head outside and make our way to the car.

Mandy looks at me with sad eyes. "That's horrible. What's

wrong with older people? Don't they know sleep is important for healthy living?"

"They believe it's overrated."

She smirks and we stop for some iced lattes and donuts on the way to the bridal shop. Since we're busy eating, we drive all the way to the shop, mostly in silence. It's too early for conversation.

When we get there, the clerk, Mrs. Petty, is waiting for us. We had to book this early on and get Mom's approval.

"Ladies," she welcomes us in. "How are you doing today?"

"Good," I reply as I grab my planner out of the book.

Mandy mumbles something incoherent and rubs her eyes. I didn't let her finish the coffee in the dorm, and made her leave the other one in the car so I didn't accidentally knock it over all these gowns and expensive material.

Mrs. Petty ushers us to the baby pink couch. On the coffee table, cream and pink macaroons sit on a silver plate. "Looks like you girls can use some coffee before we start. I have some ready if you'd like." She glances at the far end of the grandiose room.

"Oh, thank you!" Mandy replies as she heads for the coffee pot. Thankfully, the carpet is on the darker side of gray, which makes me less apprehensive. "You're an angel." She adds some specialty creamer.

Mrs. Petty smiles. "You're welcome. I have some scones too. Feel free to take as many as you like."

The white basket with vanilla scones is right near my nose. "They smell delicious."

Mrs. Petty picks up the basket and insists. "One scone won't change the dress size."

Instead of arguing, I politely take one. "Thank you. You

are too nice." After removing one, I break mine in half and pass it to Mandy, who chugs caffeine like an addict. I grab my phone, thinking of how pretty this spot would look for a few pictures, and take a large bite of the pastry, so I can photograph it. Instantly, I forget my camera. "These scones are delicious. What bakery do you use?"

Mrs. Petty's smile brightens. "Oh, no bakery. I baked them myself."

"Wow!" Mandy says. "These are great." She attempts to open up her laptop without putting her scone down, but has a hard time so she places it in her mouth to free her hands. She mumbles something, but I don't quite understand since the scone is still there. When she bites into hers, not a single crumb comes loose.

Me on the other hand? There are crumbs on my shirt. Inconspicuously covering them, I smile. "These are truly great, Mrs. Petty. I can eat all of them by myself."

Mandy pops her half out from her mouth. "Not without fighting me for them. These are my new favorite cakes. This should be the cake."

"Really?" I take another bite of mine. "I am surprised." I face Mrs. Petty. "Her favorite sweet cakes are éclairs. She even tried to convince my mother to make her wedding cake out of layered éclair."

Mrs. Petty chuckles at my comment. "I've been known to make an éclair or two."

Mandy lights up at her comment. "Do you make these every day?" Mandy asks, "I can become your daily guest."

Mrs. Petty smiles. "No, no. I was having trouble sleeping last night. Baking relaxes me."

"I am happy to help you eat them," Mandy says. "Any time

you can't sleep, just give me a call." Then as if remembering, she switches the conversation back to business. "Is your mom calling us, or are we calling her?"

"Oh, we were supposed to call her," I reply, checking out my phone. "We missed her call, but we should get one of the dresses on first." I pop the remainder of the scone in my mouth and head for the neatly colored racks of dresses. "Which ones should we try first?" We had recently narrowed down the choices with my mother, and Mrs. Petty had been kind enough to hang them on our own rack.

"These are the ones you mentioned on the phone."

I spot the gorgeous blue dress and check my hands before touching the soft material. "I'm going to try my favorite," I say, plucking the hanger off the rack.

"The one that can be worn five different ways?" Mandy asks. "Which way are you going to show? I like it short with the double-skirt style and the slit open in the front." She wipes her fingers on a napkin and touches the material. "I like this one too, in the long mermaid style more."

"You try it one way, and I try it my way. Maybe we can convince my mom to go with this one and let each girl wear it the way they like it most."

Mandy agrees, "That will save us time in trying out all the others."

Five minutes later, we are coming out all dressed up.

Mrs. Petty hands us some shoes to try with them. "The dress looks better with them, then sneakers or no shoes at all."

"True," I reply. Both of us grab the shoes and slide them on our feet. I'm used to wearing heels, so I like the added height.

Mandy's laptop gets a call and rings. "That's probably your mom," Mandy says, heading to the computer and tapping on the receive button. "Hi, Ms. R."

Mom bypasses pleasantries. She's three hours ahead of us so it's almost noon her time. "Did you girls oversleep?"

"Hey, Mom! We're here at the shop." I wave. "We wanted to get something on to show you first. How are you doing today?"

Mom's holding her phone close to her face, so I can't really see where she is. "Oh, just a little stressed, you know? It's getting so close, and it feels like nothing is ready yet."

"Well, we are going to get some of that solved today," I say. "Relax and let us show you what we got."

We adjust the computer to show us in full view. Mandy is wearing the mermaid style while I wear the double-skirt style. Both of us do a slow twirl.

"There are three other styles to this dress. So we asked Mrs. Petty to model one of the styles for us. The third style comes short, no sleeves," I say.

Mrs. Petty comes into view of the screen and does a half-circle, turns forward, then a half-circle the other way before walking away. Her runway-worthy walk shows us we need a lot of practice.

While Mrs. Petty talks to Mom, I change into a short double-dress style instead of the double skirt while Mandy switches into the short dress with a cape.

"So, what do you think, Mom? These aren't the only colors they come in. If you look at the color packet I sent you. It has all the colors on the right side."

Mom shuffles around and brings the packet up, but the scowl on her face surprises me. "These dresses are kind of plain, honey. I want you to look extra amazing on that day.”

“Mom, this isn't about me; it's about you. I don't want the bridesmaids to outshine you.”

“Well, that won’t happen.” She shrugs and goes on, “I need you to look amazing on the wedding day and the wedding rehearsal.”

I bring myself closer and narrow my eyes on her. “Mom, what have you done?”

“What do you mean?” She feigns shock and brings her palm to her chest. “I have done nothing,” she replies in a calm, muffled voice.

Aha. That voice proves my suspicions. “Are you trying to set me up again? I told you no more blind dates.”

 “It's not a blind date.” She pouts and shuts the pack. “I just invited some people to the wedding, so you can meet them.”

“People?”

“One is part of the wedding party.” She smiles eagerly. “I believe you guys will hit it off.”

Mandy offers me a sympathetic look, which Mrs. Petty echoes.

I shake my head and sit up. “Mom, it's not going to happen.”

“All I'm doing is introducing you and putting you in the same place at the same time.”

“Mom, but—”

“Already done. Just ramp up the Vavavoom.”

“Ms. R,” Mandy interrupts. “Mina’s seeing someone.”

My mouth slacks a little at the bold lie.

My mom asks, "Who is this boy? Why have you not told me about this?"

I look to Mandy to help me explain her lie better.

"She didn't want you to worry. You know, with your big day coming and all. She was planning on introducing you after you got back from the honeymoon."

"Nonsense. Bring him as your plus one. I'll make a note to add him to your table. I can't wait to meet him."

Mom points to Mrs. Petty, who has other dresses in her hand. "Now, let's see these other dresses. One way or another, you still need to look good."

———

In the car on the way to the baker, I ask Mandy, "How am I going to find a make-believe boyfriend in a month?"

Mandy makes a right. "There are plenty of guys out there."

"Someone who fits my mother's standards."

"We'll figure it out. Who knows, maybe Mr. 3B Hottie will show up and make all those wishes come true."

"Or not." Although I've often thought about him in recent weeks, he's just a what-if. Another example of how my shyness keeps me from taking an adventure. A risk. If I keep living the safe life, the introvert who hides behind social media, I'll never find someone to love me. "This is hopeless."

Mandy reaches over to me and cups my arm. "The important thing is you've got time. Finding a guy won't be an issue. Convincing him to pretend to be perfect... that may be tricky."

We stop at the bakery and grab a late breakfast. All that time trying on dresses had worked up an appetite. I ask for extra whipped cream on my cappuccino and chocolate.

Mandy asks, "We are still on for tonight, right?"

I shake my head. "I'm beat, Mandy. And I have to get some homework in. All this wedding stuff is putting me behind."

"Oh, no you don't. You already bailed on me last night and I had to go to the Sultan's Palace without you."

"It was crowded and loud." I roll my eyes, not in the mood for another guilt trip. "I have a test this week."

"You promised. And exactly! We haven't gone out much. In between this stuff and tests, we can both use some stress relief." She pouts. "How else are you going to find a guy to go to the wedding with you?"

I hate when she's right. "Okay, but you need to know I'm going under protest." I lick some whipped cream from the end of my straw. "We still have to go to the expo and check on those wedding favors for my mom, and the lady that's making my mom's jewels is there, and have I told you how much I hate weddings?"

"Not since yesterday." She smirks. "We will be exhausted."

"You're right about the stress relief. I should make an appointment at the spa," I tease.

Mandy is shocked. "A spa can't compare to hot men and free drinks at Sultan's."

CHAPTER SEVEN

The Veil

DEAN

The expo is in a closed-off park. It's been sectioned off and divided into sections. The three of us each grab a map and study the area. It's jam-packed, which I don't like. "Maybe we should just go fishing like Theo wanted," I suggest.

"Oh, no." Theo rolls the map up in his hands. "You guys wanted to come here, and shop for something to take home to Dean's mom, remember?"

Mom loves sewing. "There's an Arts section."

"Oh, check this out! There is a car exhibit. Can we go there first?" Ralph asks.

"Sure." We stand in line to get our hands stamped and walk inside, passing the rides and farming equipment. This place has booths for everything, from food to home supplies and plants and a lot more. We head to the center where the car exhibit is.

We take each time checking out the sports cars, which Ralph's drooling over. Theo's on his phone and calling me over.

I leave Ralph sitting inside a Porsche, the vendor talking to him like either of us can afford a car like this. "What's up?"

Theo pulls out one of his ear buds. "She just posted again. She's at a bridal shop."

"What?" I snatch the phone from him, racking my brain for a ring on her finger. No, she was definitely flirting with me. Or maybe, she wasn't talking to me because she couldn't. I glance at the photos to see another girl and an older woman in blue dresses. The caption *bridesmaid* underneath them.

"What if this girl is engaged?"

It would suck. "Why would she be looking for me if she were engaged?"

"Good point." He scrolls through. "Maybe she's a wedding planner."

I had seen that yesterday, but I don't confess to checking out her site. "Whatever she is. We need her for the video and to save my job, not to hook me up."

Theo chuckles. "You traveled halfway across the country on a maybe for a chance to save your job?" He pats me on the shoulder just as his phone vibrates in his hand. He pulls down the notification bar on the top of his phone.

"You follow her on her social media?" I widen my eyes at him.

"How else do you think I know where she is? I already told you I can't make a wish and rub the Internet for some magic."

"Less talking." I point to the screen. "More wish granting." I call Ralph over with a hand gesture and ask Theo, "What does it say?"

He clicks on the white tab and sees her "check-in" post. "At the expo on Rydell. That's where we are."

I pull the map out of my back pocket as he hits the screen. Immediately, I know where she is. "She's at the Bridal Exhibit."

We take off toward the south end.

Theo gives us a direction. "She's at the Jewel of Night. At least, that's what it says behind her."

"I think I see her," I tell the guys. We try to get to the area she is, but the crowds of people make it difficult to get there. And then people get in between us, asking questions and asking Theo when mine and his wedding date is. Theo takes advantage and flirts with the girls while I move forward.

"She stopped streaming a couple minutes ago," Ralph says as soon as the jewelry section pops up. But she's not there anymore.

Following the crowd, I continue searching, spotting her near another boutique, but she vanishes between the sea of people. She must be at least five-hundred meters ahead of us.

"There she goes. Down there," Ralph says. We fight the crowds again, this time trying to go across the crowd. That is even more difficult than going up stream. Eventually, we clear the bridal section and give up.

Ralph is the first to throw in the towel. "I need a break. We need to stop trying to find her in populated places."

"We came here for a gift," I remind them. "Her showing up was a chance." In the clearing, I notice two women aiming their phones at me and waving. "We got to go." I use my chin to show the guys why, and there's no hesitation. I'm going to need to get out of here faster than I thought.

Ralph flanks me on one side and Theo on the other. "Let's go back to that little coffee place. Didn't Theo say she goes there a lot? One of the IP addresses he traced came from there."

Theo bobs his head and leads us toward the exit. The coffee shop is within walking distance. On the way over, she gets another notification. "Does this girl post everywhere she goes?" Theo asks. "She's going to be at the Sultan's Palace tonight."

I don't really want to go back there, but if it means getting my life back, then I don't see another choice.

———

At the club, I can't relax. With a beer in my hand, I keep thinking back on all that's happened. Theo is talking tech stuff to a pretty brunette at the booths on the second floor, and Ralph is trying to get one of the three blondes at the end of the bar to dance with him.

I am brooding and checking out the bottom floor while giving myself an ultimatum: if I don't see her today, that's it. I'm done. I'm heading back home and asking John for a different position. Maybe I can work from the office, do less flying until things settle down.

Yet... Not seeing her makes me sad.

This girl has destroyed my career and ruined my nights—haunting my dreams. I honestly don't know why I'm looking for her anymore. My motives are convoluted.

The more I see her posts online, the more I want to get to

know her. Granted, I'm not a fan of Internet things, but she seems to enjoy posting, and talking, and filming. But I want to know what's behind the camera?

Who is the girl behind the veil of glass? The one obscuring her identity through the shutter of a camera? Because from what I peeked through the chink of reality, she's intoxicating. The shyness, the awkwardness, the kind smile and blush of her cheeks. Those things she hides from the public view, and I can't get enough of.

If I had just asked her out right then and there or gotten her phone number, all of this could have been avoided. I could have had a chance then. I could have shown her who I was rather than pretending to be a passenger.

My thoughts head down a dangerous path. I glance down at my hand.

Well, getting myself drunk isn't going to help the situation. Neither is moping around here like a lovesick teenager.

"I'm going back to the hotel," I announce to the company and take one last glance at the dance floor.

And I freeze. Dumbstruck. Lovestruck. I can't take my eyes off of her. I can't lose her again. I shove whoever's sitting next to me off the booth seat and stand up swiftly, heading down the corridor as fast as I can and glancing through the ornamental mouldings to make sure she's in the same place.

At the bar. The genie-tender's taking her order.

I rush down the stairs, careful not to topple anyone over. I thread myself through the sea of people, like a needle through silk—easy and effortless.

I'm right behind her, smelling the soft hint of anise and

amber. Her perfume is delicate and, like her, intoxicating. She's inches away from me. All I have to do is approach.

But the dumbass that I am can't think of anything to say. Anxiously, I smile and glare at the mirror, plastered on the column beside him. *No scary smile.* I tell my reflection, easing my lips down so the amount of teeth showing is not freakish.

I've been told I have a sexy smile...

Boom.Ching-ching.

Someone bumps into the shot girl standing near her, carrying a tray full of apothecary jars full of alcohol. The tray flies through the air, angling for the floor, and the poor genie-tender trips on her heels and crashes into my girl, knocking her off-balance.

I jump into action, catching her from behind and swooping her up.

"Thank you," she says with a sigh. Her eyes still closed and her breathing shaky.

I lift her back to standing position. Her back to my chest. "You're welcome."

She flips in my arms to face me. A smile broadening the horizon of her lips. "It's you," she says breathlessly.

"Hi," I say with a smile—one of the sexy kinds. *I think.*

"It seems like you're my hero again." She smiles wider.

"Lucky for me I guess."

"I'm the lucky one," she replies, still in my arms.

Theo and Ralph come rushing up. "You found her!" Ralph hoots and throws his arm around Theo. Both of them are buzzed and leaning against the mirror column.

"Wait. You were looking for me?" asks my girl.

I, of course, just nod. All this thinking about meeting her and talking to her, and this time, it's me who is speechless.

Theo nudges me in the arm, reminding me of why I'm here. *Career, not love.*

"Right. I came all this way because I need to talk to you. Can we find someplace more private?"

Ralph chimes in, "If you don't mind, miss. It's very important."

She nods and heads over to the genie-tender, who leans down to one of the bar shelves, and whispers something to him. She gets a nod and some keys in response. He looks up at the group and says, "Let me know if you need help."

CHAPTER EIGHT

Multiple Reasons

MINA

We all scurry into the room after a short set of introductions. I now know my Mr. 3B Hottie is Dean Night, but not much else. "Okay. What's with the need for privacy?" I stop short of the desk in the manager's office and turn. Right into Mr. Hottie.

All thoughts leave my mind, and I stare up at him. His eyes are so intense and penetrating me. I can't step away or focus on anything else except his hypnotic eyes, taking my breath away.

His gaze lowers to my chin, mine to his. Then up just a smidge. Those lips... waiting for me to kiss them. To meet them without fear.

"Okay!" someone to my right interrupts my chain of thought. "It looks like Mr. 3B Hottie has lost his voice, so I will show you."

He uses the desk laptop and taps away on the keyboard. I hear other voices right behind me.

That seems to snap us both back to reality. Tearing our eyes from each other, we turn toward the laptop without stepping away, his arm securely locked at my side, part of his body flush to mine.

"Did you post this?" The guy who introduced himself as Theo is visiting my blog, and that's my face on the video he's showing.

"Yes," I answer, wondering if it's a trick question.

"Great." Ralph takes a seat on the desk. "Now take it down."

"What?" I ask, now adding a little bit of space. "It's the video with the most views, why in the heck would I take it down and lose all that publicity?"

Mr. 3B Hottie, I mean Dean, explains, "If you don't, my job's on the line."

"Your job?" I ask, feeling a bit of remorse. I smooth my hair down while thinking the worst. *Did I breach some kind of law or something?* Panic takes over. "To be fair, I hadn't intended on capturing him in my shot. I was just checking in with my followers."

"We figured." Theo plops down on the manager's rolling chair. "And technically, Dean, you may still lose your job. But taking it down is where we start, getting the original down will eliminate the source, but won't fix anything."

My mind's not registering what they are saying, so I angle my upper body at Dean, who is looking at my fingers rather than clarifying. "I don't understand."

"I'm an undercover federal air marshal. Part of the Surveil the Skies program."

"Oh..." My mouth parts a little, since I don't even know what that means. "Like an air cop?"

"It's a little more complicated than that," Ralph says.

Three sets of eyes follow me across the room, gauging my actions. "So you're all air cops?"

"No. I'm the only FAM," he corrects and steps toward me. "Do you understand why we're asking you to take it down? It's not good to be a public figure. It makes it hard to protect other people if you are being stopped to take a picture with someone or answer questions or being identified."

"That makes sense." I cross my arms over my chest. "Is that why you're here?" I can't help the frown that crosses my face.

"Kind of." He lowers his voice. "I'm technically on forced leave, which I used to try and find you for multiple reasons."

"Multiple reasons?" My mind hitches on the phrase and the smile spreading across his handsome face. "Am I one of those reasons?"

He doesn't respond, not even a nod.

I step further away from him. I need to think clearly. Think of my future, my goals, what I've been trying to accomplish. I'm not saying my job is anything compared to his, but it's on the Internet. *What good will taking down my video do if hundreds of other people have reposted?*

Stop it, Mina. There's a part of me that thinks selfishly, even though I know for sure I'd take it down. Maybe we can help each other, considering my predicament.

Here goes nothing. A little quid pro quo. "I can't help you."

"What do you mean?" Ralph asks, slamming the computer top down.

I flinch at the action, but Dean seems calm, which keeps me calm. "You're asking me to lose traffic to my page. To lose followers who come to my vlog, see things, and want them. For an influencer, that's kind of like losing a job too."

"Not even on the same page as being an air marshal," Theo mumbles.

Ralph attempts to convince me. "What Theo means is you blew up this guy's life and are profiting off his disaster."

"I didn't mean to hurt you."

Dean looks so sad and disappointed, like I just crushed him.

"What if you posted that you found him since you're the one who started the search? That would help," Ralph asks.

"That wasn't my intention, honestly." To get his attention, I place my hand on his arm. "My friend took a screenshot and put out the announcement. I honestly thought it had died down."

"It hasn't." Theo stands up from the chair, comes near us, and whispers something to Dean. The other joins them.

"Do you enjoy ruining good people's lives?" Ralph asks calmly in passing.

Feeling super uncomfortable, I step away and around the table to take a seat on the office chair. A sunken feeling—a sadness—hits me.

Is it because he is no longer holding me? Or because he hates me? Or because he came for his job, not because of me? That giddy happy feeling that had flooded me before goes poof, leaving me empty as I listen to their conversation. I don't even know who says what, but most of it is about me being useless and unreasonable and selfish.

Maybe I am being a little bit selfish, but what makes his

job more important than mine? Okay, he's law enforcement, but that doesn't mean I have to bend over backward. I'm sure he can be reassigned to something else. Hell, with the comments on the Internet he could start modelling and make a fortune. Way more than I ever will.

"She's not worth your time, bro."

And that right there pisses me off. I slam my hand down on the desk. "Let me get this straight. You three," I wave my hand around, indicating them, "flew in from God knows where, searched everywhere for me, just so I could do you a favor, and because I don't jump when you say so, you think it's okay to badmouth me?"

Ralph goes to speak, but I'm not done.

So I hold my hand up in there, shutting him up. "You do know how the Internet works, right? Once something's up. It's up. I can take it down. And anyone who shared it will not have access to the video. But screenshots exist, so does free will. I'm not exactly sure what kind of miracle you were looking for, but obviously, I can't do much."

"She's right." Dean steps from between the two guys. "We are acting like selfish asshats. Sorry."

"I'm sorry too. But do you see why taking it down doesn't make sense? There will always be someone else who has it. And no offense, but my blog's been more active this year than any other year."

"Because of Dean."

I get up. Despite it being somewhat true, it was Mandy's post who got the most interaction. "I'd like to believe some people have enjoyed me blogging about my mother's impromptu wedding and how I study and plan my college life."

My eyes veer toward Dean, nailing him in place. "As pretty as your face is, it has only been on my blog once. Saying all my success has come from you seems very non-chivalrous of you." Before I give them any more fuel to attack me, I finish off with, "If you really want me to take it down and help you contact my followers, how about starting off with being nice."

"You wouldn't be losing your followers if they were following *you* for you, and not for Dean." Ralph leans against the wall, propping his foot up on the wall and leaving a footprint on the turquoise matte paint.

Dean leans back and shoves him in the arm. "That's enough." He swivels back around to me. "I'm really sorry we disrupted your day. We'll leave and not bother you again." His sadness and hurt shows strongly in the downturned corners of his eyes. It makes me want to throw my arms around him and make all his sorrows go away.

Ralph, staying true to character, asks, "What do you want in return?"

"I'll help with your problem, if you help with mine. This way we both get something out of it."

"Done. We'll help you." Dean smirks and his shoulders relax.

Theo chimes in, "Dean, you can't just agree. You don't know what her problem is yet."

They are trying to protect Dean, who is willing to help me without question, so I confess, "I am not going to ask him or you to take a bullet for me."

Just then, Mandy walks in, swinging the door open and almost smacking Ralph in the forehead. His hands swipe up and hold the door from hitting him. She glances back, not an ounce of sorry in her determined stride toward me. "The genie-tender said you were in a room with three guys."

"Do you need any help?" She whips around to face all three of them, with an energy like she is ready for battle. And a phone in her hands.

Oh, crap.

Ralph blocks his face. "Are you filming this?"

"Well," she replies. "If you take a better look..." she twirls around and ends in a pose "...you'll notice I have no pockets, so no place to put my cell."

"Excuse *Shameless* over here," Theo steps up, getting in front of Ralph, and introduces himself.

Ralph trades his stunned look for a pissed-off growl, then clears his throat and nudges Theo out of the way. "Sorry. We aren't fans of being filmed without consent." His head tilts to the side, landing his accusatory look on me.

Mandy, always the show stopper. I smile and fess up. "I'm okay, Mandy." I stand up from the chair. "Actually, better than okay. These men are going to help us with our little wedding dilemma."

"Wedding?" Dean asks. "Are you getting married?"

"God, no!" I roll out, then devote my attention to Mandy. "We're going to trade."

"Oh. Wow. They are perfect." Mandy walks to the end of the desk, then leans against it. She is wearing a short mini-skirt and a bustier top. No pockets. "Wait, trade what?"

Noticing Theo and Ralph's eyes are still on Mandy, I smile when I realize Dean is looking at me and not Mandy. Even though Mandy doesn't need a date, I include her.

"We need dates for my mother's wedding."

Dean seems surprised by my admission. "That's it?"

Mandy puts her finger up. "She isn't done yet."

Ralph pries his eyes off Mandy's chest to stare at me again. "The genies are outside, just because there are three of us doesn't mean you get three favors."

"I'm starting to get the sense you really don't like me." I scoff, and he shrugs.

"What do you need help with?" Dean encourages me to continue.

I look down for the rest of the explanation, not wanting to see rejection in Dean's eyes. "One of you will have to act as my steady boyfriend. My whole family will be there. I have no control of what they say or do. But, whoever goes as my date, will have to pretend we have been dating for a few months now. It's also out of state. So it won't be one party and see you next time. You're going to be stuck with us for approximately two weeks. No backing out."

Dean steps behind the desk, touching my shoulder to get my attention. As I am looking into his eyes, he says in a soft voice, "I'll do it."

My heart skips a beat, and I smile up at him, happy his eyes are no longer showing sorrow.

"So who is my date?" Mandy rubs her hands together.

"Me," Theo and Ralph chime in unison.

"I can make that work." She winks back at me. "Now, what is the trade?"

She's not going to like this. "Take down the Mr. 3B Hottie video."

"What?" Mandy asks.

"We put Dean's job at risk, and we are going to help him get it back."

Dean's hand slides down the back of my arm, recapturing

my attention as heat floods my body. "Thank you for understanding," he says. "Can I see you tomorrow?"

I didn't expect that. "You don't have to go on any other dates with me. We can just tell each other info over the phone."

"Yes, of course," he replies. "But we can find out more about each other in person. Besides, I would really love to see you tomorrow for dinner if you're free."

"Okay," I say. "It's a date."

His smile comes back. Infectious and gorgeous. It takes great effort to walk by him and not stay.

"Do you have her number?" At the blank expression on his face, Mandy asks Dean for his cell phone, which he surprisingly gives her. I assume she's typing in both our numbers.

"Text or call me tomorrow. We can set up a time and place to meet. See you soon," I say softly.

"Bye boys," Mandy says. "Oh. And we won't take anything down, until the wedding." As we walk out the door, Mandy whispers, "We have to tell your mom to add plus two for me."

We stop at the bar, and I give the keys to the room back to the genie-tender, and we head out to the car. I catch her up on what happened and try to avoid the guilt in my stomach.

"It's not right for him to lose his job so we can make money."

"True," Mandy answers. "Besides, we are great social media influencers. We already got the sponsorship, we just have to figure out how to keep it."

"Exactly. I'm sure we can figure something out."

"You surprise me. Who would have known you could be so tricky and sneaky?"

"I didn't know I had it in me either," I reply. "When I

found out he was looking for me because of his work, not because he liked me, I got angry. If he had asked nicely, I would have, but this way we both lose something, and both win something."

"For two weeks," Mandy says. "You are so crushing on this guy."

With a sigh, I respond and rest by head on the window of the passenger's side. "Have you seen him? He is absolutely gorgeous."

CHAPTER NINE

Cheesecake & Kissies

Dean

Despite being told to, I can't wait. Something about her intrigues me. I saw right through her attempt to get a date for her mom's wedding, but I would have said yes either way. I call her as soon as I get to the hotel room.

She answers, "Hello."

"Hi, this is Dean. I know it's late but I forgot to ask you something."

She giggles. "It's okay, Dean, what did you forget to ask?"

"Are you allergic to any food?" Seeing how that may be weird, I clarify, "I'm trying to figure out where to take you. Is there any place you would like to go for dinner?" I stop and give her a chance to answer, but after not hearing anything from the other side, I continue, "Sorry, too many questions?"

"No worries," she says. "I was just realizing no one has ever asked me my opinion before. On food choices or places to go during a date. I have my go-to foods, and I'm open to new things. I am not allergic to anything that I know of. How about you?"

"No, at least I haven't run into any. What about the last question? Any place special you want to go?"

"Nothing special. But if you are open to it, there is a place I want to try out. I have heard a lot about it, and they say the cheesecake is to die for. If you are up to it, we can go there. It reminds me of my favorite bakery."

"I don't know," I tease. "I am not usually a cheesecake kind of guy, but for you, I will make that sacrifice."

"Not a cheesecake kind of guy? That's sacrilegious," she teases back. "You just haven't eaten a great cheesecake before. There's this small bakery in New Jersey that has the best New York Style cheesecake ever made. I get some every time I go to New York to visit Mom."

Chuckling, I stretch myself out on the bed and prop a pillow behind my neck. "Let me get this straight: the best New York Cheesecake is in New Jersey?"

She giggles cutely, and yawns in between. "Yeah."

"This dessert is geographically challenged. And I have doubts."

"Don't mock it till you try it."

"You will have to take me there one day. If not, I will be forever deprived."

"Oh, no. That will be a shame!"

Talking to each other is so easy. The conversations just seem to flow from one subject to the other; we carefully evade the Internet and how it's messed up my world.

An hour later, she says, "Look at the time. Dean, we can talk tomorrow. I have a test in the morning. Do you mind if we call it a night?"

"No, not at all. I have to wake up early tomorrow too." I don't, but she doesn't know that.

"I will text you the address to pick me up tomorrow. Good night."

"Good night," I reply, waiting to let her hang up with a smile on my face.

———

After she sends me a visitor's pass, I scan the Q-code on my phone when I reach the parking lot. Security towers with blacked-out windows stand on either side, and I half expect the guard to pop out, but the divider goes up, letting me in.

Trying to find her dorm is complicated. The roads aren't labelled; some of the buildings have names, but the others do not. More than likely, I've passed it. I circle around twice before checking out the campus map at the entrance and plot out my trajectory. It's much easier to find now, and I stop my car at the main entrance of her dorm.

To get a better view of the doors and her, I get out of the car. Within a few minutes, Mina emerges, wearing a pretty floral sundress. She has this sweet and sexy look all at the same time.

Frozen in place, I'm torn with many contradicting thoughts—a darker, naughtier desire to take her back to my hotel room instead. Images of her warm body in my arms float by, and I shake my head to clear my thoughts.

I walk toward Mina, battling against my urge to make a move. Instead, I slow down as I near her. When she looks up at me, I slowly take her hand and kiss the backside. "You look beautiful."

She smiles up at me, a pink glow tinging the apples of her cheeks. "Thank you."

I keep hold of her hand. "Ready?" I point to the car.

I escort her, hand in hand, to the car, then open the door for her to get in.

"Where to next?" I ask once I enter the car.

She reaches into her purse. "I have it downloaded to my cell phone."

It only takes twenty minutes to get to the restaurant. Ralph and Theo were right, she likes to stick within the area. We pull into the busy street, and find a parking spot close by.

The spot looks pretty cool. A ramp circles the entrance, giving it two fronts: a left and a right. A small water spring fountain stands on the left side with live fish. In the middle is a statue of a woman in an old-fashioned dress, pointing up to the right side. When we look up to where she is pointing, another statue of an old-fashioned-dressed man is on a ladder holding the end of a crooked sign that says Lulu's Dinner.

I smile. "This place has character; I like it already." I hold the door for her to enter.

She smiles. "It's pretty cool."

The location is a very tactful mix of the modern and antique. The walls are packed with pictures of people from the past and old pictures of a town that used to be.

"Will it be just the two of you?" I hear someone ask.

"Yes," I say, looking down to see this petite old man.

"Follow me." He takes us to a table for two in the back, near a wall with a fireplace. "Is this okay?"

"Yes, thank you."

I pull out the nearest chair for Mina to sit and take the seat opposite.

Almost immediately, a young perky waitress comes by. "Hi, I will be your waitress. Here are your menus." She distributes them to each of us. "I will be back to get your order."

We peruse the menu in silence. A few minutes later, she returns with bread, butter, and two glasses of water. "Have you guys picked anything yet, or know what you'd like to drink?"

Mina orders a peach iced tea and I order a Sprite. I flip the page of the menu, looking for the dessert section.

Mina sighs and places her menu down. "They have a lot of wonderful choices here, how can we pick just one?"

"The only thing I know is I don't want fish."

"Why not? These dishes look good to me?"

"The guys convinced me into fishing. I left at two p.m. with no fish and an earful."

Mina giggles. "I see, you are punishing the fish for not letting you catch them."

"Yes, exactly." I close the menu. "I think I will go with the steak."

"Sounds good. I think I will go with spicy shrimp in garlic sauce. Although, the salmon looks really good as well."

The young waitress returns to our table. "Need a little more time?"

"No," Mina responds. "I will have the spicy garlic shrimp, and he will have the steak."

She turns to me. "How would you like your steak, sir?"

"Medium rare."

After the waitress disappears, we busy ourselves with small talk. Mina asks me to tell her about the fishing trip, so I tell her how we rented a boat and fishing gear. That the boat had a GPS set to some local fishing spots. "It was Theo's first time." I chuckle. "The face Theo did when reaching for the bait was very comical. I don't think he knew it was a bag of live worms before he sunk his hand in it."

"Gross!" Mina's smile increases. "I would have loved to have seen it."

"You would have gone fishing with us?"

"Of course, stinky fish are way better than taking a two-hour-long exam any time. How come you guys didn't catch anything?"

"Oh, the guys caught fish. I didn't."

Our food arrives amidst laughter, and we dig in.

I continue my story and talk about my friends. She prods me for questions on them, but seems to get tense at the mention of Ralph. He was hard on her yesterday, but he's a nice guy. Soon she'll see that.

By the time the waiter comes back, we've abandoned the food, both of us almost full. Getting lost on her sweet voice and the ways she giggles is easy, and the way she talks about dessert has me craving for something sweet. "I'll get this boxed up for you." The waitress grabs our plates and steps away for a minute before coming back. "What would you like for dessert?"

We had already discussed this. "I will take peach cobbler, and if I am correct, she'd like your famous New York cheesecake."

She nods her agreement.

"Would you like coffee with that?" the waitress asks.

Mina responds, "Yes, please."

"Two coffees," I correct.

As soon as the waitress leaves, Mina says, "I have no room for more food."

"Neither do I, but it would be a shame if you came here to taste some cheesecake and walk away without it."

"True. That would be a shame."

When the desserts come, they look wonderful and huge.

Mina exclaims, "Wow. I didn't leave this much room."

The waiter smiles. "I will get more containers in a moment." She pours some coffee into the coffee cups, then places a small container of sugar and a small bowl of creamers near it.

When the waitress leaves, I ask, "Does it look like the one from New Jersey?"

"Yes, very similar."

"Go ahead, taste it, I can't wait to find out."

"Only if you taste it with me. Like this, if it's not good, we can both be disappointed."

"Okay, together then." I lift my fork and scoop some of her cheesecake.

We both take a bite.

Mina hums in bliss, distracting me from the cheese and sugar in my mouth. "Yeah..." She uses the fork to point at this food. "This is pretty good. Definitely taking second place. The one in New Jersey is still the best, though."

I smile, as she takes a second bite. I love watching this girl eat and moan to cheesecake.

I point to the peach cobbler, after I shove some in my mouth. "Would you like a bite of this one?"

We both go in for a taste of the peach cobbler. "Not bad," she says.

"Not bad," I agree. "But I like your cheesecake better."

She places her arms around her cheesecake in protection. "I will share the rest, only if we get me another one to take home."

It's a deal. We finish the cheesecake and the coffee.

The waiter comes back with the containers. I ask for the bill and another cheesecake, to go.

When we get outside, it's dark. Twinkling lights everywhere, giving the entrance an enchanted garden look.

Mina gasps. "It's so beautiful. I want to take pictures."

"Would you mind if I go place these in the car?" I ask, lifting our leftovers for her to see.

"Not at all. You go; I will be here."

When I look back, she's taking pictures of the statue in front of her. Returning, I see her standing on the railing and leaning over, snapping pictures of the fountain.

I approach, slowly enjoying the view. She looks at the photo and adjusts her angle, still standing on the railing. She leans in even closer for another picture. Her foot slips from the bottom railing, and I catch her just before she goes over.

"What is it with you and climbing?" I say as I swing her into my arms.

She smiles and hooks an arm around my neck. "I like climbing. It's the falling I could do without." She drops her phone in her lap to straighten her dress and tug on the hem, making sure she's not flashing anyone. "Thank you for catching me."

"No problem? I love rescuing beautiful women."

"Oh, you do? Have you rescued many beautiful women?"

I don't mention the videos that got me in trouble. Since we seem to be tiptoeing around that. "One so far, but I have rescued her a few times now. Can I count her as more than one?"

"Absolutely not."

I smile back. "Did you get it? The picture?"

She grabs her phone. "Yes, I got it. Let's go over there to get the statue with the sign."

"Okay." I throw her over my shoulder and carry her to the other side, careful not to let her dress ride up.

"Dean, this isn't exactly what I meant."

"I have been waiting forever to get you back in my arms. Do you think I was going to let you go so quickly?"

"I was just in your arms yesterday," she says with a giggle.

This is the only time we're alone. "Like I said, forever. An eternity of waiting for you to kiss me."

She leans in. "An eternity is a very long time." Her voice softens while she gets even closer. With her lips just an inch from mine, she whispers, "What if that kiss doesn't come, what then?"

"That's simple," I say as I bring her lips to mine and kiss her, drinking her in like a man who has been dying of thirst, and her soft lips, warm mouth, and playful tongue are the fountain of life.

A phone rings, breaking the kiss. "Do you have to get that?"

Mina replies breathlessly, "I think it's yours."

"Oh. Then it can wait." I kiss her again.

The phone rings again. This time, she breaks the kiss. I lean my head to her forehead. "I think you should check that."

Securing her with one arm, I use the other to reach in my pocket for my cell. "Hello."

Theo's rushed voice threatens to ruin my night. "We got to go back home."

I glance at the pretty girl, hanging on a railing. The one who was just hanging on my every word. "You have bad timing. Can't this wait?"

"John says it's urgent. I'm booking us a flight."

"Fine." I hang up to find her wide eyes on me.

"What's going on?" she asks.

"Work stuff."

"Trouble?" Her voice sounds sad. "Because of me?"

I hold her chin up so I can see directly into her eyes. "I'm with you today. It was all worth it."

She smirks. "It's a shame you're leaving."

"Not till tomorrow. But we do have two weeks, right? And lots of phone dates." I pull her toward me.

She leans into my body, placing her hand behind my neck. "It's too bad you have to leave tomorrow."

"Then tonight will have to do." I kiss her, crushing her body to mine and capturing her soft moan between my lips. I increase the intensity, pressing my lips to hers a little bit harder until the door to Lulu's opens and patrons giggle.

She reluctantly breaks the kiss. "I guess we should leave."

"I don't want to," I admit.

"Me neither." After I ease my grip, she steps back and holds her phone up. "Can I take a picture of us before we go?"

"Only if you send it to me, and don't put it on the Internet."

"Deal. Say cheesecake *and kissies*." She stretches out her arm and takes an *usie*, with her in my arms. I repeat the first part, and do the second part.

CHAPTER TEN

Double Trouble

DEAN

Theo and I sit on the chairs, watching an angry John rant and rave while pacing back and forth. There's nothing I can do, but listen.

"She already took down the post," Theo jolts in when John mentions it for the umpteenth time. "I checked just now."

"She did?" We both know she said it was her leverage. She'd only take it down once I played her date at the wedding. Maybe she had a change of heart.

He holds his phone out for me to see. "I checked before we got on the red-eye, and it was still up."

Pinned to the normal spot is a picture of a cheesecake in a take-away box from Lulu's. Underneath, it says, 'Had the best time, and I'm already missing the sweetness of their peach cobbler.' *She means me.*

John stops walking and snaps his fingers in our direction.

"You have two more weeks. If all of this doesn't die down, you're fired and there's nothing I can do for you."

The blow doesn't sting as much.

"And, Theo, you can join him on leave."

Theo almost drops his phone. "What?"

I make the mistake of asking, "Why is Theo getting punished?"

"He knows why."

Theo shrugs and confesses. "I may have used databases I shouldn't have to trace down the original poster."

"You hacked the government?"

"No." He shrugs. "I just logged on as John."

This sets John off on another rant, for another hour. It ends with, "Stay home and out of trouble."

After we leave and clear the building, Theo turns to me and asks, "So... I'm pretty much moving in with you."

"Uh, no." I laugh at his attempt. "Theo doesn't do well with free time."

"If I get fired, you better make room for a roomie because my landlord is only nice to people with boobs. So either I need to get some, or I need to keep my job."

I shake my head as we walk to the car. We had driven from the airport together. "I think we'll figure this out. Mina took it down. When I get back there, I'll ask if we can do what you suggested about being found and giving the followers an ending."

"They prefer happy endings," Theo says. "And I doubt she's going to do that until we get to the wedding, but maybe she can use her platform as a way of giving them a happy ending."

"What are you talking about?"

"Most of the people who commented were women." Out comes the phone again. "See," he asks as he scrolls. "And what do all women want?" I'm glad he doesn't wait for an answer because I've got no clue. "A fairy tale. Which you can give them. Take a photo at the wedding and have her blog about finding you."

"Uh." I glance back at the building. "Didn't you just hear John? I'm supposed to stay off-grid, not plastered on screen."

"Yes, but curiosity is fueling this search. If you end it, give them a story, then no one will care anymore."

"Or not."

"Why do you always have to be so rational?" He tucks his phone back into his pocket and reaches for the passenger side door. We get in, and while he talks about how I shouldn't go back to California just yet, I think about his theory. And honestly, at this point, I'd try it.

For every day during the week, Mina and I talk for hours. The three-hour time difference isn't even that bad once we get used to it. We've talked about her hopes and dreams, about her mother and the wedding—which she really does hate, along with the bridesmaid dresses—and we talk about our friends and cheesecake. That girl can have whole conversations about cheesecake, unless she's eating it. Then she's just moaning deliciously.

I called her about twenty minutes ago, but she didn't answer so I decided to try again after lunch. To kill time, I'm barbecuing in the backyard.

Ralph drops by, using his key to get in. He descends the

stairs to the backyard, rubbing his palms together and licking his lips. "Nice. Steak! I'm hungry."

"I wasn't expecting visitors, so if you want some, you're going to have to go to the grocery store and grab another steak, but you're welcome to grab a beer from the ice box."

He pops back in the house and grabs one. "I'm surprised you're still here. Every time I come over, you're talking to Mina or talking about going over there."

I shrug and flip my steak. It's big enough to share. "The last time you were here, you were talking about dreaming of Mandy." I throw back at him and flip the peppers and roasted pineapple.

"Yeah, but I don't know."

"Do not tell me you're chickening out about the wedding."

"No, no not at all. I can't wait to see Mandy again." He sits in one of my lawn chairs. "I just found out some info and thought you should know."

"What information?"

"What's this?" he asks as he picks up my new phone, changing the conversation.

"It's my new cell." I take it back from him. "What info?"

 The doorbell rings. "Can you get that, Ralph? This is almost done."

"I left the door unlocked. Theo said he was coming over."

Sure enough, Theo pops into the garden, holding a pizza. "Did you tell him?" Theo asks Ralph, cutting straight to the point.

"Tell me what?" I transfer my steak from the grill to my plate, then go for a handshake.

"Not yet," Ralph pinches out.

At noticing them both eyeing my steak, I say, "I'm not

sharing my steak, just letting you know that from the beginning. If you want one, I can add some bricks and keep the fire going until you go pick one up from the store.”

“No worries, I brought a pizza and beer. The brothers were packing when I pulled up. I took the last spot on the street.”

I pause a piece of my steak just an inch from my mouth. I place my fork with the steak still on it back on the plate. “Why is everyone coming over today?”

Theo replies, “We found out some info about the party, and you're not going to like it. You are probably going to want to back out.”

“Me? No way. I promised Mina, and I’m not going to leave her hanging.”

Theo reaches for my steak, and I smack his hand away. “I found out whose wedding we are going to.”

“Mina’s mom's wedding.” I grab my new phone and pull up the food delivery app, and order some BBQ from the local grill for all of us, then grab the bread. If the brothers are coming, we may as well do this potluck style. I slice the steak thinly and make sandwiches while Ralph gets up and heads inside, probably for some condiments.

Theo opens the box and sets it beside the platter on the outside table. “I mean, who is Mina’s mom marrying?”

“Who cares.”

“You should. It's some rich dude. High in the media's eyes, which means lots of press. Lots of fans, and if Mr. 3B Hottie is there, it may cause some issues. You know, with your job.”

I stack the sandwich rolls on the plate and take a seat. “So, it's my girl or my job? My choices suck.”

“Pretty much.” Theo swipes a roll from the plate and sits

back on the lounge chair, resting his feet up. "What are you going to do?"

"Weren't you telling me to do the whole wedding thing and post a pic, giving a fairy-tale ending?"

Theo licks his lips and shouts back into the house. "Bring the mustard!" When he finishes chewing, he shrugs. "One picture, one person is different than the media. You might as well walk a red carpet."

It's not like I had much hope for resuming my job anyway. "I can ask for a different position in the office."

"A desk clerk?" Theo laughs. "You know nothing about computers. I mean, do you even know what's the latest version of Word?"

"I know what Word is, asshat. Maybe I can train the guys, or something. I didn't technically breach protocol, that's why they haven't officially fired me."

Ralph comes back in with the State brothers, who had met with the food delivery guy up front.

"Someone say party, *manito?*" Robert leads the group with the food in his hands. Hernand and Ralph are speaking in hushed tones in the back.

"Stop making fun of Dean and get your asses over here before the steak gets cold and the beer gets hot." Robert ushers as he drops the bags on the table and fist-bumps me. "I hear you're a lovesick teenager or something." He flashes me his pearly whites and uses his thumb to hike his brother into the drama. "He said, not me."

"Said what?" Robert says as he sits on the opposite end of the table, near the pizza.

"About his girl." Theo had already scarfed down one sandwich, and he's on a second. "We were just catching him up on the news."

Robert and Hernand share a glance, telling me there's more to the story. For all of them to be here, something is up.

"What are you two doing around here? I thought the new security business was keeping you busy."

"It is," Robert says as he grabs a slice of pizza. "We had a new job. It's a big one."

Hernand says, "We were going to say no to the job, because we don't have enough people to pull it off safely. That's why we're here. We were hoping you guys could help us out as a sign-on. It's good publicity for us, and we can make sure to keep you out of the public eye, especially because we need someone with your kind of experience to pilot the private planes."

Ah. That's why they are here. "Wait. He's the client who lent us his plane?"

Robert bobs his head. "No. That would be your other future father-in-law. He's one of our biggest clients."

Guess I owe him a favor. "Well, I'm free from my day job, probably for the rest of my life. Count on me if you need me to have an extra hand. I'm your man."

"Thanks," Hernand says. "But it's a little more complicated than that."

"How complicated can it be?" I ask.

"It's Judge Reed," Hernand and Robert say simultaneously. "He's being targeted for his high-profile case and is looking for some extra protection for him and his family."

Theo takes over, "Wait. I've heard of that name." He takes out a phone and runs a search. "Well... Guess what Mina's last name is?"

"Reed," I say.

"So, your client's Mina's father?"

"And the protection is for his daughter while she's in New York for her mom's very high-profile wedding." Hernand takes two slices of pizzas and flips them on each, making a calzone-type sandwich.

Theo grins goofily. "The world isn't so big when we're all connected by the Internet."

CHAPTER ELEVEN

Piloting Her Heart

Dean

The next day, thanks to State Security's client list and Mina's wealthy family, I flew a private jet back to California. I entered the cockpit feeling a little anxious and worried, then my tension evacuated and it was just me, the plane, and Theo as my passenger.

I had forgotten how good it felt to see the sky from the nose of the plane, to cut through clouds and steady the metal in turbulence. It's beautiful up there. The vantage point is the world, and up there, the possibilities were endless.

If only it were that easy to steady a person, to hold on and ease through hardships.

I have a feeling turbulent times are ahead. Apparently, Mina's reluctant to being protected, insisting on her freedom. And when one of the men watching over her in Cali saw me picking her up and kissing her, of course Judge Reed ran a background check and did his digging. Half of me thinks this is why John was so pissed off, but I'm not going down that road.

And I'm not going to keep this from her. That's no way to start a relationship or help one last. Plus, people are easier to protect when they know they are being watched. It's not always necessary to let them know who is doing the protecting, just that they are.

We check into the same hotel as last time. Immediately, Theo gets to work doing some tech things the brothers asked him to.

But I can't wait to see her and hear her voice, so I call her. "I have a surprise," I say as soon as I hear her say hello.

"Hmm... You're eating cheesecake?" she guesses.

"Close..." I joke. "I'm in town and would love it if you would go out to dinner with me."

"Really? I'd love that. I'm free in about twenty minutes. I just have to send in some things to my professors."

We talk for another five minutes while she makes herself some coffee. When we hang up, I shoot Theo a message and take the car to Shrayar University. The whole way, I feel like a kid again.

When I get through the gate and park the car, I wait by the front door for my date to come out. Stressed. Nervous. Pacing back and forth. Trying to figure out how to broach the subject of working for her father, in a way, unnerves me. I swear I'm sweating and look down to check for sweat spots.

None. Good, at least my body is working with me on this. Feeling a presence near me, I turn mid-pacing and stop in front of her. She has this big smile on her face and a twinkle in her eyes.

I smile back at her. She closes the gap between us and kisses me. All the stress and worry slip away as I kiss her back.

"Hi," I say after we break the kiss. "Are you ready?"

"Yep, where are we going?" She curls her arms around me and looks up at me.

"It's a surprise."

———

She seems confused but smiles as we get out of the car. It looks like we are in a quiet suburb town. "Where are we, Dean?"

Happy I found a place where she hasn't been to or heard of yet. "I had to ask Theo for help."

She scrunches her nose at me as we take a small walkway in between two properties. It leads to a beautiful garden that is open to the public. "What do you mean?"

"Well, someone mentioned this place on the flight we met on." I rub the place that had the now healed scratch. "Theo cross-referenced. He had previously mapped out all the places you had posted about or checked in at when we were looking for you." I lead her to this old house with a welcome sign in front of some stairs leading down to its basement.

"Yeah... Still weird. I'm waiting for it to be a cute story on how we found each other."

We descend the stairs, as I fill her in on how. "A lot of investigating, hard work, a little bit of hacking, and a lot of wishing on genie-tenders."

She snorts a laugh. "I mean, it gets cuter if you spin a positive light on stalking."

At the base, a host welcomes us. I give him my name, while she snaps a photo, but pouts. "No cell service."

"Exactly why I chose it."

The host calls someone to take us to our table, and we enter the opulent restaurant with hanging chandeliers. She's awestruck and therefore silent until the waitress returns to take our orders.

She breaks the silence just as I'm about to spill my guts. "Wow, this place is incredible."

"I have to tell you something important."

She arches her brow. "I hope you don't get angry with me."

"Shoot," she says. "I don't think there is anything you can tell me that can get me angry with you."

She is so beautiful. I want to keep her happy and smiling all the time. But, she has to know; it will come out eventually.

"Well, come on," she says. "Don't keep me waiting. My mind will just jump to possible scenarios that can be much worse."

"I work for your father."

"What!" There's a flare of her eyes as she searches for something to hit me with.

"Wait. That came out wrong. Let me explain."

"Good idea." She crosses her arms over her chest and leans back in her chair.

"He called two of my best friends, who happen to own a security company, for a job, and since I'm temporarily in job limbo, I work with them."

I see the anger behind her eyes as she tries to hold her temper. "What job?"

"Protecting you."

"Did you agree?"

"They explained the situation, and you're at risk. The cases he's presiding over involves bad people who are sending him death threats, even pictures of you."

"I am not going to stop my life every time someone threatens my dad," she blurts out. "This is why my mom left him. He's controlling, and if he could, he'd lock us up and shield us from the whole world."

It clicks. "Is that why you started vlogging?"

She narrows her eyes on me, but relents and rests her elbows on the table. "I couldn't go out into the world, so I brought the world to me."

"But you realize how your blogging puts you in jeopardy? Anyone can look at your feed and—"

"Map out my common hangouts?" Harsh eyes meet me again. "I live my life the way I want to, and neither you nor my dad will change that."

"I know. That's why I want to help you finish your last semester. Protect you. I'm not trying to hide you."

"Oh," she says, all the furry leaving her eyes.

I wait to see if she will ask for more info, but she doesn't. "Mina, the threat to his life and yours is real, you know that, right?"

"I've been threatened since I was two, and here I am." She reaches over the table to pinch my forearm. "Still alive, and no one has come after me. I've been doing good all on my own."

"You haven't been on your own. Your dad had someone follow you. That's how they knew about me. Half of me even thinks they were on the plane the first time we met because my friends knew him shortly after. Which means, I didn't even notice."

She sighs, her chest rising and falling as she digests that comment. "So what do you want me to say here?"

"My friends are helping your dad and getting help for your family. Your dad said your mother's fiancé is covering protection for her and the wedding parties, but he wants to make sure you're safe."

"That's where you come in?"

"I'm already going to be there with you."

"What about the media coverage? I was going to tell you not to worry about coming with me because I didn't want to make your job situation work."

"I don't care about my job right now." I grab her hand gently and kiss it. In a low voice, so as not to scare her or anger her, I say, "I want you to let me protect you."

She is quiet. I see it on her face—her eyes—she wants to say no.

"Please," I say and kiss the inside of her hand again gently, and then another. "Please," I whisper into the palm of her hand as I kiss her again. I look directly into her eyes. "I can't lose you," I whisper. "It took too long to find you. Let me try to keep you safe."

"Fine."

A sigh of relief escapes me. She turns the hand I'm holding to grasp mine, and she smiles slowly. "How could I say no when you ask it that way?"

Her stomach growls. Her hands leave mine and go to cover her stomach.

As if on queue, the waiter comes with our food. I giggle and lift my fork up. "Maybe we should eat before my stomach growls louder than yours."

CHAPTER TWELVE

Naked Thoughts

MINA

After dinner, we stroll through the park before heading back
to the car. He was so intense back in the restaurant. If I had
said no to letting him protect me, he'd think I don't trust him
and we'd break up.

I couldn't take that chance. So, I said yes, just to make
him happy, not because I think I need any protection. I'm on
the opposite side of the country; it's not like anyone would
come looking for me.

"Dad is the one who needs protection, you know? Not
me." I break the silence. "I'm all the way on the other side of
the country. Besides, isn't this guy in prison until the trial?"

"People don't need social media to be influencers. Money
and fear are very persuasive motivations. And he threatened
you directly. Your dad doesn't want to take any chances with
your life, and neither do I."

I smile up at him. "So, what's your plan?" This path's lit up with standing light lamps, illuminating the floral patches around us and the benches in tactfully discreet areas.

"We're working on that," he replies. "I spent the whole night thinking of getting to you, and how I should approach the subject. I honestly didn't know how this would go, so I never made any plans."

"Great start…" I giggle and point to the bench. *These shoes are killing me.* "Good thing it's spring break soon, huh?"

He takes me by the waist and escorts me to the seat. "I missed you."

I smile up at him, then lean in closer to rest my head on his shoulder. "Did you come back because you wanted to protect me or because you missed me?"

"Both." He rests his chin on my forehead.

"I've thought about you every day," I admit. "Long distance is a little complicated, but I'm almost done. I have one semester left. Flying gets expensive."

"Well, if I get my job back, then I'll be in Cali a lot. We do a lot of flights to and from here."

"And if not?" *I messed that up for him.* Mom's marrying rich and my dad has plenty of money, but it's not mine. They pay for college, and I work for my things. I'd have to pay for each of those flights back, or trick my mom into thinking I want to hang out with her.

"Then we'll figure it out together. We do have the wedding in New York."

"Don't remind me. Mom's driving me crazy. I kind of wish spring break was cancelled or that I can get away right after the wedding."

"Isn't she going on a honeymoon?"

"She says she's too old for one." I sigh, hating that we are talking about my mother. "On the bright side, you'll be there. And since you're protecting me... it means I get to see *more of you*, right?" My tone delves from my gut at the thought of seeing him without clothes on.

"Right..." Sobering up a little, he picks up on my slip. "So, during those thoughts you had while I was away... have you *thought* of seeing me naked?"

Heat rises to my cheeks, and I bury my face closer to him so he doesn't see me turning the color of a tomato. "Once or twice."

He lifts his cheek up and turns me to him to see the answer blatantly spread across his cheeks. He lowers his lips to mine and gently kisses me. Stopping, he hovers close as if there are more kisses to come. Instead, he whispers, "That can be arranged, you know?"

"What?" I whisper back.

"For you to see me naked," he replies. "Any time. Any place."

"Is that so?" I smirk, feeling the warmth pool in the center of my stomach. "Mandy's art class has been looking for a naked model. I will let her know you drop trousers *any time. Any place*." I get up to add space. Naked bodies don't belong in parks.

He catches my wrist, and his lips tempt me closer. "Only if you're the only one there." He releases my hand and crooks his finger. "Bring those beautiful lips back over here."

"We're in a public park."

"An empty one." He looks around.

Sidestepping, I run for it. I make it about fifty feet before he catches me, tightening his arms around me.

Our bodies make contact and heat spreads through my body, certain parts of me tingle with excitement. As he wraps his arms around me, our bodies rub together. My breath catches in my throat.

Swooping into his arms, he whispers in my ear, "My offer is for you alone. No one else, whenever you are ready."

"Guys are always ready," I mumble as I wrap my arms around his neck, and lightly kiss him by his ear, continuing a trail down to his neck.

"Keep doing that, and I'll be ready right here."

With his help, I shift to wrap my legs around his waist, anchoring myself to him. His breath catches, and he throws his head back. Encouraged, I continue my line of kisses on his neck, then out of nowhere, I lick in a circular motion, tasting him.

He growls and backs me into a tree, our bodies rubbing closer together. His masculinity presses against my body. He moves his hands to my legs, caressing and slowly raising my dress as he continues to kiss me hungrily.

I break the kiss as a loud moan escapes from me.

In the distance, a car door slams shut. The bubble we had created around us dissipates, and the haze clears up. My legs are no longer wrapped around him; my dress is lowered but I am still against the tree, his body still touching me. His hands around my waist.

"I'm sorry," he whispers. "I got carried away."

I lean in to give him a gentle kiss. "I did too. Think anyone saw us?"

"I don't think so." His eyes peer into mine, traveling

through the depths. "It's difficult for me to release you and step away. I am mesmerized by you." He leans in close enough to kiss me; his body once again flushed against mine. He stops himself and kisses my forehead instead. "We should go."

"Why?" I tease.

He winks at me and tugs on my hand. "I think I need to give your mind a little bit of something to hold on to."

Oh... "Move faster, then."

————

The phone blasts me out of the most peaceful sleep. I wake up in his beautiful, large arms with drool. This man had me salivating all night. I quickly wipe my mouth and his chest dry and grab the annoying phone. Why is my mom calling me so early?

I rise out of bed, slide the button to answer the call, and tiptoe toward the bathroom while my mom runs off a checklist. "Mina, have you checked in with the favor vendors? They haven't arrived yet and my jewellery got here last night. I specifically asked for one blue stone to be placed in the setting, now I have nothing blue, and despite your wisecracks about my husband being my something new and me being my something old, I have made other arrangements. Your father graciously provided the something old, more damn drama in my life, and my something new? More bodyguards."

She takes a breath, and I fit in a few words. "Morning, Mom." I lean against the counter, staring at the toilet, debating whether or not to pee while on the phone.

"Morning? It's noon for you." She shouts. "Are you just

waking up... Oh. My God. Your flight leaves in fifteen minutes.”

“Shit.” I glance at the toilet and hit the mute button, knowing she’ll go off on this. I can’t argue with a full bladder.

“It’s fine,” she says to my surprise. “I’ll see if I can book you another flight out. Everything is mostly done. Or I can ask for the private jet. We’ll figure something out. Hold on a second.” She disappears, not even realizing I’m not answering her. When she comes back, I had successfully peed on the phone, with none the wiser, and brushed my teeth. “The jet is in California.”

A knock on the door comes before he carefully swings the door open. Mom had been on speaker phone so I bring my finger to my lips, telling him to be quiet.

“I guess he knew you’d mess up. Lucky for me, my future husband always thinks ahead. He just sent a message to the pilot who flew it over.”

Dean raises his phone up to eye level, and I arch my brow while holding in a smile. Dean types away and I’m guessing what he says is being relayed to my mother.

“He says he can have the plane ready to go in a few hours, Mina. And I’m assuming Mandy—”

“Oh, shit!” At my outburst, both Dean and my mom glare up at me. “She texted me last night and I told her to meet me at the airport.” I flip through apps on my phone to see twenty messages.

“Well, at least one of you is responsible,” Mom huffs out. “How do you oversleep when you know I’m getting married and the rehearsal is tomorrow morning?” She lets it go. “Get your stuff and come here. The dresses are here so you don’t even need stuff. Just come over. When you get here, don’t be alarmed by the security or the press. Security knows who you are and your father's help insist on not leaving your side, so you're set up in the West Wing."

She hangs up, and Dean, my pilot, has another thing in mind.

CHAPTER THIRTEEN

Yacht

Dean

Theo stays behind an extra day, which means I didn't get to do much talking on the plane, but we did have a little fun before takeoff. When we get to the mansion, Mina's sequestered by her mother, and I'm being debriefed and called into meetings on how things will go down. State Security's main focus is Mina.

Screw my job and staying out of the spotlight. There are plenty of other things I can do to make money, one's that don't involve modelling or anything like that. The State brothers have offered me a permanent position, one that gives me more flying time. I had forgotten how freeing flying could be.

It does, however, mean I have to tell John I quit, which will not go down well. John was the one who got me into this job. He's the one who's been helping me, and now I have to tell him that I give up. Fighting with the Internet is a battle I can't win, and there are better things to do with my time, like being with Mina. Protecting her. Loving her.

By the time we finish our briefs, it's late and Mina's asleep. So I go to bed in the room reserved for security and shoot Theo a message telling him about the change in plans. He's more than likely on a flight back, so when he lands, he'll know the wedding got moved to the yacht for security reasons.

———

The next day breakfast is sent to the rooms. We all get ready and go down for the rehearsal. As I patiently wait for the girls, someone knocks on the door. I answer to find an uncomfortable-looking Robert at the door.

"Hey. What's up?"

He comes in and shuts the door. Even though this place is huge, he whispers, "There was an attempt on Judge Reed this morning."

"What?" I rub my head as I reach into my suitcase.

He takes a seat on Theo's side of the room, the one reserved for him. "He doesn't want the family to know."

I nod in agreement. "Is he okay?"

"Shaken up, but in confinement. Ralph and Hernand are with him now, but he keeps insisting on them being here. Mina got another threat."

"Another one?"

"This one came with photos of her boarding the plane, at a park with you, and at a restaurant. And of her friend."

"We were being followed?" I didn't even know.

"From a distance, but yeah. The judge asked his ex to move the wedding, but she's not having it."

"From the little bit I heard about her, she's not the most reasonable woman."

"That's putting it nicely." Robert tosses one of the pillows in the air, just as Mina walks in without knocking.

"Oh, my God. Can we get—" She notices Robert is here with me.

He smiles, noticing I am still absorbing her beauty. "Hey," Robert says. "You must be the young lady who stole Dean's heart."

I smile. "This is Mina. Mina, this is Robert. He is the one who will be escorting Mandy since Theo and Ralph are busy."

"You are?" She smiles and glances at me. "You two wait here. I will check if she is ready."

Within minutes, Mandy barges in, fidgeting with her bracelet that can't latch. "I do not need a babysitter. You can go," she says, not noticing who she is talking to.

Robert stands and grabs her wrist with one hand, stopping her. "Let me," he says in a soft voice.

Mina comes to my side, I place my arm around her as we both watch quietly.

Mandy looks up to see him for the first time but says nothing as he fastens the sparkly thing around her wrist.

While swirling his finger on her wrist above the bracelet, Robert softly says, "I am not a babysitter, just a man who would be honored to be the date of a beautiful woman."

"Flattery is nice, but it's still a no." She glances at Mina. "We've been fine without you. This place has more security than the White House. I think we'll be fine."

Robert reaches into this pocket and produces his cell

phone. "Last night, did you notice anyone watching you when you went to visit Theo at the hotel?"

Both mine and Mina's eyes bulge, and Mandy's about to lunge at Robert's throat.

"It wasn't me," he answers. "Someone is following you two and the threat isn't just for Mina anymore."

Mina sighs softly and urges Mandy to agree with some silent girl code, which falls on blind eyes. "Mandy, we don't have time to argue."

Mandy narrows her eyes on Robert, who tucks his phone back into his tux pocket. "If you ask me, I think the only reason you two are here is because you were accompanied. Didn't Theo take you to the airport?"

Mandy huffs the steam from her head out in short puffs. "That's none of your business."

While the two argue and flirt with each other, Mina smiles up at me and steps closer as I lean in to kiss her. She feels my gun strapped to my side and lifts my dress coat for a better look. "What's this?" she asks.

"I am carrying today. I'm not taking any chances on your safety."

Mandy overhears us and asks Robert, "Are you packing?"

Robert smirks. "Way better than Theo."

She scoffs and smirks while he lifts his dress coat slightly. "You're welcome to search me."

"I'll take your word on it." Mandy swivels on her heels and turns to Mina. "I don't feel like hearing your mom arguing today."

"Right. And we still have to introduce my um... boyfriend." Mina winks at me. "Maybe, we'll just tell the truth of how we met."

The girls walk toward the door, which Robert opens for them. Mina steps through first, smiling for me to follow as she hooks her arms through Mandy's.

When we near the crowd, I approach Mina and give her my hand.

Mina directs us towards the family members we haven't met and introduces us. Then her mother catches us and gushes. "Here she is, this is my daughter Mina—she is my maid of honor—and her partner." Her mom has no clue what my name is.

"Dean." I extend my hand to shake the woman's hand. "Mina's boyfriend."

Mina's mother arches her brows at my title. "To be honest, I thought Mina was lying to get out of being set up."

"You didn't." Mina's mouth drops open, forgetting pleasantries.

"Yes, but I'm sure there will be plenty of other women for them to meet." Without much more, the mother and her coordinator step away to another group of people.

"What was that all about?" I ask.

"Mom's trying to set me up. She never cancelled the dates."

"Well, they're cancelled. I don't plan on sharing you with anyone tonight."

———

After about four hours of repeating steps, everyone is ready for a change and food. The vehicles arrive to take everyone to the yacht. Upon arrival, security guards escort us inside after checking us off a vetted list. At the top, we are greeted by a waiter and a glass of champagne.

"What's wrong?" Mina asks, noticing my tension.

"We are too open," I respond. "This is beautiful, but if anything is going to happen, it might be now."

Mina tenses and starts looking around. "They followed Mandy too." The thought had not left her. "What if they were trying to take her?"

"She's with Robert," I remind her and grab her as she is about to step away and bring her close, hugging her from behind. I whisper in her ear, "Do you see anything wrong?"

"No," she responds.

"So we wait, and I will hold you here, in my arms, stealing as many kisses as I can." I kiss her behind her ear, and her neck a few times, before we hear Mandy and Robert arguing.

"Will you stay close? I don't want you to get hurt," Robert says.

"I can take care of myself," she says as she keeps dodging him and walking away.

When everyone boards, Mr. Hughes, Mina's new stepfather, asks his head of security to ask the captain to start the cruise and invites his guests to mingle and join them below deck in a few minutes.

By now the whole crew is here. I spot Hernand, Theo, and Ralph around the deck. Two of them are acting as servers, the other as part of the crew. The ear piece I slip into my ear connects all five of us, but there's not much talking going on. We all have tasks, which Robert is completely failing at.

"What is Robert doing?" Hernand asks in my ear.

I chuckle as he weaves through the crowd after Mandy.

Mr. Hughes approaches the sidelines, where his escorting security crew is stationed. He seems worried.

Hernand notices the interaction and approaches Mr. Hughes.

"Mr. Hughes, is everything all right?"

"Something isn't right. The boat should have been moving."

The next comment from Hernand is to us. *"Keep your eyes open. Theo?"*

There's no answer.

"Where's Theo?" he asks.

"Last I saw him, he went below," Ralph answers.

I stiffen. Theo was in charge of background checks on the crew. *"Something is not right. I'm going down to check on him."*

"Theo is not responding," I advise Mina, who's looking at me with gaping eyes. "We should tell your family." Slowly, as if nothing is wrong, we head to Mandy.

Mina whispers the situation, which gets Mandy to stop fussing over being followed.

On the way to the bride, a servant stops us and asks, "Would you like some appetizers?"

"No," I say, holding Mina close.

She replies in a politer tone, "No, thank you." Then side steps around him, aiming for her mother.

When she releases my arm, a server approaches her mother from behind.

Platter in one hand, gun in another. Eyes on my girl.

On instinct, I tackle the man, bringing him down to the ground. While wrestling, I hear some commotion from behind.

And the sound of a gun going off.

Mina screams so loud I let go of the man on the floor.

Another attacker had grabbed Mina from behind, trying to drag her away.

Another gun goes off.

The one in front of me.

The man gets pummelled to the floor by Robert, and I glance down. The warmth is spilling from my gut.

CHAPTER FOURTEEN

Fired Up

Mina

In the Hospital, the State brothers wait for the results. The news is playing in the background, reporting on injuries and telling the timeline of events.

I sit, nervously waiting as Hernand paces back and forth. "What's taking so long? Can't they send someone out just to let us know he's alive?"

A random person sits near me and Hernand glares at the young guy, cradling a bandaged hand to his chest. The young man understands he'll be used as a venting method and immediately moves to another seat.

I stand up. "I'll ask again."

Hernand replies, "Good idea."

He follows me all the way to the desk.

"Name, please," the lady says without looking up.

"Dean Night." I sigh as the adrenaline starts to wear off and make everything so very real.

"There's no new information at this time."

"May I speak to the hospital administrator, please."

"No."

"Why not?"

"Because you do not need him to come tell you the same thing. The answer is still going to be the same."

Hernand gets angry. "If she wants to talk to someone, you get him. I don't care if he is home in bed."

I place my hand on Hernand's shoulder. "Give me a few minutes." I quickly text my stepdad. The one who has been calling me nonstop.

In less than ten minutes, someone comes rushing out with a phone in hand. "I am so sorry, sir. Yes, of course, sir. It won't happen again."

He walks straight for me. "Sorry for the mix-up." He leans to whisper something to the nurse, who goes red in the face.

"How did you do that?" Hernand asks.

I point to the name above the wing. "The Hughes wing."

Hernand smiles.

The nurse disappears through the ER, and the administrator says, "What can I do for you?"

"It's been hours and no word. My boyfriend came in unconscious and barely breathing. There were some security personnel that came in as well. We still know nothing about any of them. My family is waiting. And the hospital staff won't tell me anything because I'm not family."

"Do you have all the names of those that came in?"

Hernand passes him a piece of paper with all the names.

The admin nods and picks up a phone at the station and reads off the list. Once he's done listening to the other end, he hangs up. "Okay, let's start with the boyfriend. Which name is that one?"

"Dean Night," I reply.

"He is currently stable; his breathing has improved. He hasn't awakened yet, so we are sending him for some tests to make sure nothing has happened to his lungs. And some cranial tests in case something happened there."

He continues with the other names. I'm feeling woozy. Hands grab me before I fall to the floor.

Hernand walks me to a chair. "Mina, are you sure you weren't hurt?"

"I don't think so. I'm just overwhelmed," I reply.

The administrator interrupts, "Why don't we get you checked out?"

"No, I'm fine," I insist.

"Can I get you anything while you wait?"

"Coffee, please."

"And food. It may be why she is feeling lightheaded."

"Of course," the administrator says. "I will get right on it."

<hr>

A few hours later, we are both in a room with a still sleeping Dean. He had woken up but started calling out for me, then passed out again. Hernand kept Dean's mom informed, and we've been informed Theo is awake and doing okay.

"The shot to Dean's chest could have been much worse," Hernand says into the phone, eyeing me as if he thinks I'm going to burst out in tears. "Fractured ribs, no collapsed lungs, which is good. They removed the bullet in surgery and are working on reducing the swelling and pain so he can breathe normally."

"Who are you talking to?" I ask.

He covers the phone and whispers. "John, Dean's boss. Or ex-boss at this point." He holds a finger in the air and returns to the call. "We don't know for sure. He is on painkillers and anti-inflammatories. If everything goes well, he should wake up and be able to leave in a few days."

I move closer to Dean and curl my hands around my bent knees. I'm so tired but I don't want to shut my eyes.

"Theo's going to be okay. They found him below deck, heavily medicated." Robert continues as the door opens. Theo walks in, arm in a sling.

I rush to him and hug him. "Thank God you're okay."

"You are a sight for sore eyes," Robert says as he taps him on the back, putting the phone on speaker so John can ask how he's doing.

Theo answers, "I won't be typing for a while, but I am well."

"That may be a good thing since both of your faces, identities, and information are all over the news. I'm glad you guys are doing okay, but you're both fired."

The conversation goes on and on but I tune it out to look at my Dean. How frail he looks with the gauze around his torso and the machines attached to his nose. He's breathing fine.

If I hadn't met him, none of this would have happened. I wouldn't have gotten him involved, I wouldn't have ruined his life, and I wouldn't have made him Internet Famous.

Tears well in my eyes.

But I also wouldn't have fallen in love, and I'd probably be dead by now. At least they caught the guy, and the trial is over. The guy ordering the shots got shanked earlier. He had bled out in solitary confinement. Too bad that didn't happen before he ruined my mother's wedding day.

"Hey." Robert's hand lands on my shoulder. "He's going to be okay."

The question is will *we* be okay. *Will he still want me when he wakes up? Will he hate me?* I shake the thoughts away, knowing that's not me. Those are my fears.

"I know."

"I have to talk security stuff with Theo for a bit and call Mandy."

"Right." I glance between Theo and Robert, the mention of Mandy made both of them very tense. "Tell her I'll call her when he wakes up."

"Okay," Robert agrees. Both of them leave me behind with my phone, that I don't even want to touch. We were going to post that we found each other and end the suspicion, but it doesn't even matter now.

"Dean?" I call out, placing my hand above his. "You know the doctors say you just need time to heal... I am here, and I need you to wake up." I kiss him lightly on his lips. "I love you."

"Good..." he whispers in a husky tone.

My eyes jump to his, but they're wincing from the pain. "You're awake."

"I'm also in pain," he grimaces as he tries to move.

"Let me call the doctor!"

"Wait!" He stops me in place. "I love you too."

"You'll love me even more once I get you some meds."

The End:
Subscribe to the Hotness

Meet the next Internet Famous Celeb in SECONDS.

INTERNET FAMOUS COLLECTION

Whether they accidentally rose to fame or staked the claim, these modern-day princes are social media royalty. Follow the Internet famous celebs as they deal with fame, power, and the consequences of falling in love. Each story is a STAND-ALONE fairytale retelling with an HEA and swoon-worthy alphas. There's a little something for every book craving.

✓Sonya Jesus's twisted retelling of Cinderella brings to life a fairytale killer obsessed with a True Crime Blogger and her Internet famous crush in SHOOK.

✓Mel Walker livens up the stage with his Princess and

the Pea retelling, which combines music and dance into the beat of love. STAGEFIGHT.

✓Nancy Chastain's friends-to-lovers, sports romance, BEAST, follows the MMA fighter and his first love in a page-turning Beauty and the Beast retelling .

✓Tasha Lewis's Little Mermaid retelling follows the prince of the ocean on his shipwrecked voyage in DESERTED, a contemporary romance that gives love a voice.

✓Maree Moon's Arabian Night retelling combines sweet romance and accidental fame, turning the Internet into the genie of love and romance into a chanced encounter. CHANCED.

✓Cam Johns's dark retelling of Rapunzel is a second chance romance that will leave you craving more from this hot celebrity chef and salivating for SECONDS.

✓Jade Royal's lesbian romance changes up The Legend of Hua Mulan, defying the rules of gender identity, war, and the Internet by a girl more DEVOTED to win than her contenders.

✓MK Moore's Snow White retelling is a steamy contemporary romance about the gamer celebrity and the girl who TROLLED him.

www.rewrittenfairytales.com

Get More Info:
www.facebook.com/rewrittenfairytales
Subscribe to the Hotness:
http://eepurl.com/gYEHqL

www.ingramcontent.com/pod-product-compliance
Lightning Source LLC
Chambersburg PA
CBHW020258180726
47994CB00028B/2441